MISS VEAL AND MISS HAM

Vikki Heywood

MUSWELL
PRESS

First published by Muswell Press in 2025
Copyright © Vikki Heywood 2025

Typeset in Bembo by M Rules
Printed by CPI Group (UK) Ltd, Croydon CR0 4YY

A CIP record for this book is available from the British Library

ISBN: 978-1-83834-010-0
eISBN: 978-1-73919-306-5

Vikki Heywood has asserted her right to be identified as the author of this work in accordance with the Copyright, Designs and Patents Act 1988.

This book is a work of fiction, and except in the case of historical fact, any resemblance to actual persons, living or dead, is purely coincidental.

Extract of lyrics from Something On a Tray from
After the Ball (1954) by Noël Coward used by permission of
Alan Brodie Representation Ltd www.alanbrodie.com
With thanks to the Noël Coward Foundation and The Noël Coward
Archive Trust.

Muswell Press, London N6 5HQ
www.muswell-press.co.uk

Our authorised representative in the EU for product safety is Easy Access System Europe, Mustamäe tee 50, 10621 Tallinn, Estonia
gpsr.requests@easproject.com

For Rosemary Manning

Chapter One

Twelve-year-old William Hodge whistled some stupid tune his mother often sang into the silent mouth of the letterbox. The notes floated out from between his teeth, yet despite his careful aim they drifted away, muffled by the dawn mist hugging the lane. His normally impressive whistling seemed the best thing to try, having failed for some time to conjure up at least one of the two old hens who ran the shop by banging on their front door.

He preferred Miss Ham with her crusty powdered nose, scented hankies and sweet treats. Miss Veal was the watchful one, long-necked and eagle-eyed, she missed nothing; though, unlike most of the kids in the village, William had his reasons to keep in her good books. He could hear the hum of the early morning traffic, winding its way along the new arterial road into High Wycombe. The autumn chill penetrated his school blazer; his thin cap had slowly deflated onto his head in the damp. His mum told him to wear the school jumper she'd knitted for him, but it was way too big and full of lumps and anyway it got him teased rotten; all his pals wore shop-bought ones.

The old hens were really old. What if they were both upstairs dead in their beds? What if it was a double murder?

Or one had strangled the other and then stabbed themselves with a knife? Beaky Miss Veal would surely be the one to murder the flowery Miss Ham, yes, that's the way round it would be. Or Miss Ham might have choked on one of her gobstoppers and Miss Veal died of a heart attack trying to extract it with her long bony fingers.

William bent down and peered through the letterbox, his eyes scanning the slit-shaped view down the dark hall and the staircase beyond. Could he spot a glimpse of ankle, or feathers, floating in the stair well?

...Tripped and fell, caught her neck in her own dressing gown cord, and with the other dying of the shock – all very sad –and our poor William was the one who found them ...!

William sat down on the bale of newspapers beneath the shop window, recently flung from the delivery van on its way past. He rubbed his cold round face; he was at a loss as to what to do – Miss Ham said she needed him to come early and help move some stock in the cellar and he wanted that sixpence. He dared not bang on the glazed shop door; Miss Veal would take umbrage at such an act when it was clear to see the blind was down and the shop closed. There were many rules to life in the post office and sweet shop; though the front door of the little house only two short paces to the left, it was the one to use if the shop were closed. *Holding on to decorum,* as Miss Veal would say, was William's constant struggle, his failure to comply always eagerly noted and retribution swift.

Upstairs, Beatrix Veal woke with a start; she could hear someone banging on the front door directly beneath the bedroom window. Her fingers reluctantly crept from the warmth under the coverlet to find the bedside table lamp and flicked the switch. She leaned across the large lump in the bed beside her and pulled the alarm clock face from the other bedside table close to hers – good grief – the hands said quarter past six. She prodded Dora, whose helmet of curlers prickled the eiderdown, and hissed into her ear, as if her voice might carry to the street below.

"Wake up! Dora, wake up! It's quarter past six for Lord's sake. Someone is at the door. I thought you said you would set the alarm. Shake a leg!"

"Oh ... I'm sorry ... I told William to come fifteen minutes early today ..." Dora said, from under the covers.

"Why didn't you set the alarm when I asked you last night? I knew I should have done it but, oh no, you would have it your way," said Beatrix, dropping her feet to the bedside mat, which only just masked the chill of the lino. She raised the sash window wide; she did not lean out but called.

"William? It's Miss Veal here. Please hang on a tick and I will be down," she said, lowering the window to six inches above the sill. Beatrix was all for fresh air. She slipped out of their bedroom, as she did every morning, to dress in the back bedroom. She had a quick wee in the pot under the permanently made-up single bed, then a brisk rub down at the sink with a flannel, brushing her teeth with an efficiency born from over sixty years of practice. Lucky to have most of them; she would hate to be like poor Dora, whose porcelain 'twin set' spent silent nights suspended in a pink solution in a glass by the bed. She dressed quickly into the clothes she had laid out the night before; brassiere, pants, girdle, stockings, slip, blouse, skirt, jacket, stepping last into her brown lace-ups.

She moved to the dressing table. Her steel-grey hair was shaken from its night plait tied with a ribbon, then brushed several, rather than the usual hundred times. As she worked, she considered her reflection with its mouth full of hairpins and wondered if someone would still find her striking; a rare moment of self-regard. She knew the answer. Stringy old maid. Her gaze lifted, drawn by the brightness of the departing full moon; its sharp reflection picked out the frost on the roof of the hen house at the end of their small garden, highlighting the chalk lines that dusted the peaks of the ploughed fields beyond. The night frost had silver-plated the view – greying out the warmth of last afternoon's late autumn bronze; a chilly night the hens would have had of it.

She gave her face the lightest brush of rouge on each cheek, a dab of powder to nose and forehead to take off the shine – nothing more. Seams straight, brooch and watch on. Hanky in jacket pocket. Done. As she did every morning, she bent down and flipped over the little ivory day calendar on her dressing table. Thursday 18th October 1951. *Forgive us our trespasses as we forgive those who trespass against us* – though rarely said since school the words of the Lord's prayer jumped into her mind unbidden. The quiet before the storm; tomorrow the bailiffs would come.

As Beatrix left the back bedroom with her pot in her hand, she found Dora hovering on the landing clutching her own, lifted from the commode in their bedroom, the folds of her nightgown still warm from their bed. She was holding on to the bannnister, looking tired and wan. In the last few months a gradual decline had dramatically speeded up for Dora; her ten years ahead of Beatrix, which used to be an irrelevance, now mattered.

"I'm sorry about the alarm clock, Beattie. I clean forgot. I asked William to come early today and get a bit of a bob for a job. I wanted to have an excuse to give him a tip. I'll be down in a jiffy." Dora's myopic anxious stare revealed she knew she was in trouble. Her weak smile affirmed, without

4

much to show for it, that she would get things back on track just the minute she had located her spectacles.

"Get dressed dear, then come on down and put the bally kettle on." Beatrix knew this thin comfort. Today of all days, she should be kind, but she felt as brittle as her words; for months she had felt dull, no worse, sullen and though she could see how much it reduced Dora, she had lost the ability to overcome the depression caused by her inability to control events. Besides, in thirty-four years of running the village post office and sweet shop they had never missed being awake by six o'clock and her dressed, downstairs, and ready for the thump of the newspaper delivery on the shop door.

Beatrix descended the stairs, carefully balancing her two liquid charges, down the thinning red floral Axminster runner Dora insisted on splashing out on when they first moved in . . . *They will appreciate it just as soon as we open the front door, dear* . . . she turned left down the passage, unlocked the back door, and deposited the pots of wee in the outside wash-house. Hurrying back, she passed through the scullery and into the little shop, converted by the previous post office tenants from the front room of their two-up two-down. She moved swiftly between the two counters, to the right the sweet shop counter, to the left what was still referred to as the post office counter. The entire space traversed in twelve efficient paces. She snapped up the blind and the electric light flooded out though the glass-panelled door into the dark street. She could see William peering in through the words etched on the glass, *Post Office and Sweet Shop – Madams Veal and Ham.* She lifted the snib on the latch to unlock the door and the doorbell jangled. She worked hard at a smile.

"Good morning, William. Dear me, we are running a

little late this morning. Would you bring in the newspaper bale and put it over here on the post office counter for me? Thank you dear. Well ... done. I'm not entirely sure what Miss Ham had in mind for you to come so especially early today. We need to get on with the papers now, but would it be possible to come back another time? What a bore for you I know, might that be possible?" She saw his crestfallen face, little knowing this would be his last day in the job. Dora was right about finding a way for a tip.

"Let me see. How's about this for coming on time as you were asked?" Her voice sounded guilty, she was almost gabbling, as if he was a sweet rations inspector catching them on the hop. She moved to Dora's till and rang it open. There was the sixpence Dora had wanted to give. Beatrix shoved the coin into his cold hands.

"Shouldn't I do the job first?" he said, suspicious that this unaccustomed generosity in her meant some kind of penalty for him.

"Oh, don't worry about that dear," she snapped back, taking her wafer-thin flat steel knife from behind her counter and slicing the string on the bale; newspapers spilled out and in her haste most of them slid onto the floor. William bent down and started putting them back, but she pushed the whole lot to the ground with a cry of "just let me do it boy ... please!" and he stepped quickly away, repelled by her vehemence. She grabbed the red string dispenser and her black marker pen from the counter and got down on her knees to sort out those that were for his morning delivery, marking each with a name, street and house number and tying them in bundles if more than one item. It being Thursday, the *Bucks Herald* for Mrs Hodge, William's mother, and to feed her knitting obsessions *Woman and Home*; *The Express* and the *Daily Mail* for Terry Longhurst, their landlord and the horrendous weekly *Tit-Bits* for Muriel his wife; the *Telegraph* for Mr Martens the verger and *Today's Woman* for his wife; *The Times* for her friend and early closing day walking companion, the gentle Oliver Cope; *The Manchester Guardian* for poor Mr Rickmansworth, who lost his wife and couldn't seem to get on top of things; *The Daily Sketch* for the vicarage; and the whole assortment of options for Phil and George at the pub and Mrs Gibbons at the tea room. She was quick, she was efficient and only just in control as she sorted the titles through blurred eyes – never late, never late and now this mess today; the day was not supposed to be like this, today she needed it to be the most ordered of days – damn it, damn it, Dora.

She looked at her watch. Just after twenty-five to seven. It was more than time the boy was going. She must say something to break the silence her loss of self-control had created and welcome him back into the role of her assistant.

"Now, William, we are getting somewhere, aren't we?" she said, standing up and straightening her skirt.

The lad stepped forward with his bag and she piled all the bundles into its wide mouth, though he was more than capable of doing it for himself. William hoisted the bulging bag onto his shoulder and opened the door; the doorbell jangled as he collected his bike from the flint stone wall.

"Thanks for the sixpence, Miss Veal. I'll come back tonight ... if you like ..." he said, preparing to cycle away.

"Oh ... no ..." What to say? Perhaps suggest another time? "William don't come back this evening please!" she called out to his spinning back wheel.

She lowered the blind – hoping that no one had passed

7

by and seen her scrabbling about with the papers on the floor with William standing idly by. She flicked the door latch snib to locked. What a terrible start to the last day.

Beatrix wiped her brow. No sign of Dora yet – always a slow starter. A morning radiance like hers was never quick, or simple, to apply. She looked at her watch again – there was still plenty of time to get things back on track before opening up at eight o'clock. She began to move the papers; back and forth she went, between the floor, the counter and the newspaper stand, moving on automatic, scanning the headlines as she worked.

'GENERAL ELECTION – TOO CLOSE TO CALL?' said *The Times*. Though Attlee was a fool, Churchill was a spent old drunk of a man. 'Britain Strong and Free' was his headline slogan – with endless leery carping about 'the need to maintain our traditional ways of life'. Try living my traditional way of life, Mr Churchill; just you try it, she thought. *Elections are a lot of fuss about nothing* – her father's voice in her head, dismissing all politics, but Beatrix and Dora marched for votes for women so 'fussing' was in their nature. Though they had been slow starters, they became enamoured with the importance of the cause, or perhaps more accurately, the possibility of the success of the cause. Increasingly educated in the ways of dissent and the refusal to accept the status quo at tea parties with friends, or friends of friends, they graduated to watch from the rear the braver souls throwing eggs at passing politicians. Eventually they found their place and a particular pleasure in handing out leaflets as the women's suffrage marches passed them by down the Strand. Strictly a pre '38 pastime, throwing an egg – you wouldn't catch someone wasting one in the Second World War. Far too valuable.

They were both a good deal quieter these days – all active political passion spent after two world wars. When did their pessimism start? An informed observation of the reality at the end of the Second World War, so different from the First, destroyed any optimism of a better, more liberal, or more equal, world; man's inhumanity to man and woman seemingly a relentless burden. Now they merely grumbled from the side-lines, bitter after all that hope. Churchill would beat pathetic Attlee, and, like the autumn mist, the election would come and go leaving life in the village just the same; perhaps, after wanting to challenge him one way or another all her lifetime, she had to admit her father was right.

The stand filled and the shop shipshape, she passed through the door at the back and into the dark scullery. The embers from the stove had kept the little back kitchen and the shop warm overnight, and though they badly needed shaking into life to heat more than a kettle, or cook more than some toast, they would have to wait; it was important to get things back on track upstairs.

She found Dora sitting on the bed, still in her bed jacket. The room felt chilly, so Beatrix struck a match on the grate; the gas fire popped and began to glow. There was nothing like a gas fire to cheer a room, though its heat barely penetrated much beyond the fluffy pink rug before it. Dora chose the rug on a trip up to London; Dora would. Though dismissive on the day the rug arrived, Beatrix had to admit a growing appreciation, no, more than that, a fondness. She would kneel on it in front of the green tiled hearth to dry her hair and, in days gone by, they would strip naked and make love on its wool and nylon mix, their bodies glowing as the blue-tipped gas flames crept up the Bakelite.

"Everything all right?" Beatrix said, sitting down on the edge of the bed next to her public companion, her heart's secret.

"It's too much like hard work this morning and you are right to be cross with me, I know it, but what's the point really Beattie? And besides, I can't find my specs." Beatrix looked around and spotted them slipped down the gap between the bed and the base of the bedside table. She rescued them from the floor and handed them over; Dora looked up, sighted again, and asking for forgiveness.

"I'm not at all cross," she said and took Dora's hand; always warm, but the touch so light it had no substance to it at all. Useless bloody hands, never could open any-thing: bottles of pop, jars of jam, tins of biscuits, turning keys and opening windows were all a trial and had to wait for Beatrix's brutal grasp. Grabbing life by the throat wasn't Dora's way; life grabbed at her, and she claimed her nerves to be defeated by the shock on a regular basis. Until recently Beatrix was of an altogether different view – life was for the grasping. Although she still tried her level best, her ability to play her old part and overcome life's hurdles, beat all comers, was now lost, leaving her furious with herself at her own impotence and resentful of her lot. None of this was any help to poor Dora; today was a day for making amends.

"Let me sort your things," Beatrix said. "Perhaps you got out of bed too quickly? You really were fast asleep. Take it slowly."

"Actually, I might have taken two of my sleeping pills, rather than the usual single one last night by mistake, and they've made me rather fuzzy."

"'Might have taken two by mistake?' Truly?" Beatrix laughed. "Dear heart, I wouldn't blame you one bit if you had taken two quite deliberately. We are both scared out of our wits. I couldn't get to sleep myself."

"Well, perhaps I can be forgiven for wanting to be sure of a good night's sleep. You should have said. I would have given you a pill, or even two. If I'm honest, I wish now I had taken the ruddy bottle," said Dora, untangling her hair net from the bristles of her curlers.

"What and left me with none and to face the bailiffs alone? Thanks a bunch," said Beatrix.

"Don't worry yourself on that account. I have made sure we have more than enough," said Dora, her fingers feeling their way along until she found the hairpins holding her curlers, which she began to remove and place on a small tray on the bedside table.

"Poor Doctor Cohen . . . putty in your hands," said Beatrix, placing Dora's favourite mauve cashmere cardigan, her frock of purple silk and her underwear comprising a brassiere, stockings, stays and silk bloomers beside her. She retrieved the black button-back shoes from under the bed, their heels higher than strictly sensible for someone of nearly seventy-four.

"Shall I dress you?"

"No, let me be."

"That's the ticket. I'll get the kettle on and for goodness' sake, don't forget to put your teeth in."

"Ha, ha duckie . . . very droll," said Dora, brushing out her tired grey curls.

Beatrix was filling the kettle from the tap in the scullery when there was a loud rap on the shop door. The ferocity of the banging made her run to unlock it – surely she had not forgotten someone's paper and William returned? As she lifted the latch Terry Longhurst pushed the door wide with a severity that matched whatever crime it was that he needed to report. His mottled cheeks were puffed up from the cold and his stupid tight moustache twitched. The bell quivered against the open door.

"Good morning. It occurs to me now that if you had kept earlier hours, you might have had a business worth saving . . . get more customers on their way past to the early bus – see?"

"Very possibly. Can I . . ."

"Thought you might have done a runner from the bailiffs . . . but the papers turned up this morning!"

"Here to the bitter end Mr Longhurst, whatever that might be . . ." said Beatrix, smiling and holding her ground so he could not pass the threshold.

"Typically, Miss Veal, there's been an error."

"Why, I am so sorry. I do hope William apologised; he may have been a little late today."

"It's not that. I have been given the wrong paper . . . *The Manchester Guardian* . . . when you know perfectly well that I take *The Express*!" He left out *my dear woman*, but it hung like a bad smell between them.

"How absolutely terrible. Please do let me change it at once." Beatrix hoped the mockery in her excessive apology would sting him, but she doubted he had the intellect to notice. Damn it; doubtless this would confirm to him, if more evidence were needed, that their inability to cope was at the root of all their financial problems. That their coming eviction was a self-inflicted wound after the GPO sold him the property in '49 – at a knock-down price no doubt. Beatrix knew – and she knew he knew – that once her official sub-post office role was removed, the shop alone would never turn a profit, even if sweet rationing did finally come to an end after this election. The fact was they were sunk. She grabbed *The Express* from the rack.

He snatched the newspaper from her hand. "Muriel's kept the *Manchester Guardian* . . . for interest. I don't expect there to be any extra charge."

"No of course, please do have it, take it as a final gesture."

"Of goodwill you mean? I notice you have not asked me to settle our newspaper account with you, I trust that is not how you have managed all your debtors. You must know it wasn't me who called in the bailiffs, that was the bank. I would've been just happy to get the property back. Never wanted any fuss."

Terry Longhurst put the paper under his arm, and to her horror, he ushered her aside and stepped over the threshold – the act of which made Beatrix's hair rise on the back of her neck, like a cat protecting its territory. This insufferable man was the epitome of the bad manners found in the new world order, his aftershave overpowering, and he gave no consideration to removing his pork-pie hat.

"I don't expect you to ever appreciate the point, Miss Veal – but there was a far more honourable way out of this mess for you both. You should've taken the chance to leave with the compensation I offered after I bought up the shop from the GPO. You could've chosen that path," he said, looking round the unaltered shop as if searching for something.

Beatrix sighed. "Is this in an any way a useful conversation for either of us to pursue?"

"Probably not."

Terry Longhurst's watery eyes hovered over Dora's counter. The sweet jars looked down on him, their backs straight, their glass chests puffed out. "What gets me in all of this was why you ever thought the bank would extend the agony and give you more time to pay back your debts. I remember your face when you told me two years ago . . .

right proud of yourself you were . . . that the rent was going to be covered and not to worry. As I said at the time you didn't have the trade."

"I think the extension was denied to us out of a failure by our bank manager to adhere to the old-fashioned concept of common decency. We should have been given more of a chance."

"Well, that, and the fact that your bank manager is the very much wiser son of the old man who turned a blind eye to your troubles over the years."

"To my mind loyalty is never a crime."

"Nothing wrong with that Miss Veal. Favours are what makes the world go round, but they are always in return for something. I don't blame the older party . . . I just can't understand it. To my mind it only put off the inevitable and increased the pain to all. Anyway, as you say, water under the bridge now, ain't it. Not much sign of packing up is there? You plannin' on doing a runner tonight? Wouldn't blame you . . . that's exactly what I would do in your position."

"I don't think that is remotely any of your business." Beatrix held the already open door as wide as it could go, in the hope that even Terry Longhurst would not be so rude as to remain. He stood his ground, eyebrows raised, requiring an answer.

"I can assure you, we will be here when the bailiffs come to collect what they can," said Beatrix, after a long pause. Though it was not a lie, as they planned to be here even if their souls were absent, she would have preferred not to have been forced to say it. "I presume someone from your office will be here to collect the keys?"

"They most certainly will. I'll probably ask Miss Moyle to pop over on her way in to the office tomorrow morning, to save you any humiliation. Unless ... that is ... you care to give me a set now? It would be very regrettable if the bailiffs have to resort to breakin' in, they always make such a mess."

"That won't be necessary. Miss Ham and I will make all the arrangements perfectly. Now if you don't mind ..." Beatrix bowed her head and gestured with it to the door.

"Keys?" he said holding out his free hand.

"I'm sorry?"

"Why not hand them over now Beatrix? Then it's done, and we won't be having to bother you tomorrow."

"Mr Longhurst, I don't expect you to understand this, but suffice it to say the notion of you having a set of keys to my home, a place that remains my home until tomorrow morning ..."

"Not that you've paid for it for some time ..."

"... my home for the past thirty-four years would be utterly abhorrent to me and to Miss Ham. Enough. Please. Enough. It is all over tomorrow morning and enough is enough. Now go. Good day."

"Have it your way, as you always wish it so. Like I said, remember how this situation has arisen. Whatever happens tomorrow, the way that it happens will be entirely your choice." And he tipped his hat and left.

It most certainly will be that, was what Beatrix dearly wanted to scream out loud to his retreating back. She leaned on the door and opened her mouth as wide as she could, releasing a long stream of breath, a forceful sigh. She wished she could conjure up from the depths of hatred within her all the sand of the Sahara Desert and blast him with her hot breath into a pile of dust.

Beatrix grabbed the door and slammed it hard shut with such force that it flew back open. She banged it again – and again for good measure. Most satisfying. The bell jangled off its rockers, the movement of air oxygenating the poisoned atmosphere as the door swung back and forth like a bellows. Out of control. She hoped she might smash the glass onto his stupid tasteless disappearing hat; the man was nothing but a spiv – *our bête noire*, as Dora called him. Beatrix felt wild – but what good did being wild do? She must get a grip, get a grip. She gave the door a couple of hefty wafts, which sucked wisps of mist into the shop, before shutting it gently. She stroked the poor glass, grateful to it for holding its own so well; she flicked the snib on the latch to lock it, she untangled the string on the sign from the wound-up blind, which both reverted to their usual closed positions. The jangled bell relaxed back on its spring. This was her castle and she would defend it.

She moved to behind the old post office counter and unlocked her drawer, going through the motions of opening up what remained of the post office. She set out her books of stamps, her letter weights and her weighing machine, cash tin, pad of ink and the wet sponge; the weighing of letters and the sticking on of stamps represesenting the last part of the old role left to the ex-postmistress. She stroked the smooth wood worn to a shine. In days gone by her customers would rest their parcels here before her weighing and stamping. She paid in and handed out their savings and cared that their letters and packages reached the front line for two world wars; once she had counted – she had been a vital link in the chain – but now her contribution was to make way for others. She put her forehead down on the counter's cooling surface. Stretched out her slender arms as far as they would go. She felt her ribs rise and fall, rise and fall. That error with the newspaper was highly regrettable.

There it was. If she could get Dora to stick to the plan, it would be the last day of regret.

Before she closed the drawer, Beatrix pulled out the letter she had written last night to Oliver, here at her counter, in the yellow gloom of the shop electric light, as Dora slept the sleep of the drugged overhead. She looked again at the envelope. She passed quickly through the back of the shop into the scullery, down the short hall, through the front door and was outside before any reconsideration could interfere with her purpose. She turned left and paused in front of the round red letterbox that stood outside the shop, tapped the envelope twice on the back of her hand, twice on the top of the red post box, then pushed it into the gaping mouth. Beatrix looked up and down the road now beginning to clear of the mist: no one in sight. She stooped to pick up the milk bottle; it was ice cold to the touch, reminding her the bally kettle was still in the sink. Through the doorway she could see Dora finally descending the stairs in her crabwise and clinging manner, dressed, made up, and ready for the fray. To be fair, she had tried hard not to overdo the slap today, which was gratifying as the reduction was for Beatrix's sake, yet it was still an impressive mask.

"Who was that at the shop door?" Dora asked, following her slowly into the scullery, with a degree of conspiracy that was not entirely necessary.

"Terry, I messed up his paper – what an idiot . . ."

"Yes, ghastly man."

". . .I meant me."

"Don't let him poison everything, Beattie." Then, after a pause, "It gives him far too much pleasure."

"He pushed his way into the shop, asked why we hadn't sent a bill to settle up ... asked why we hadn't started packing."

"Oh, good Lord, what did you say?"

"Nothing much – I can't remember."

"Surely you can remember what you said? How did you make him leave?"

"He asked for a set of keys. To save the bother tomorrow."

"What did you say?"

"Stuff it – or words to that effect. Do you want the wireless on?" Beatrix asked, in the hope of avoiding the potential for any further conversation.

"No thanks," said Dora. "I'll help get breakfast sorted. Let's push the boat out and have our favourite marmalade."

"Let's," Beatrix replied, wishing she could sound less tight-lipped, less scared. Sticking to the routine when everything was so upside down today felt forced, but necessary. Steady to the last. She turned away and put the kettle on the stove for that much delayed morning cuppa.

"You might want to go check on the hens, Beattie? You look as if you could really do with some air," said Dora.

"No. Let's have breakfast."

"OK," said Dora, looking desolate and sinking into her chair by the table. Beatrix moved over to be close to her.

"I am sorry I was cross, but why did you ask William to be here early today of all days?"

"I told him to come and help move things round in the cellar."

"Why on earth would we need to *move things round in the cellar*?" said Beatrix, her heart feeling strained, her head heavy. She sank down on the other side of the small wooden table; she held her chin in her cupped hands to prop up her tired head and stared at Dora. Something was shifting, she knew it, but what? She should not have posted the letter to Oliver without checking.

"In preparation for the ordering of the fireworks, of

18

course," said Dora, her eyes down, examining the old green oilcloth.

"What do you mean in preparation for the ordering of the fireworks?"

"There is no call to be so sharp and repeating everything I say, Beattie." Dora's beady eyes darted upwards to meet Beatrix's stare and pushed back hard. "This relentless belittling is exhausting. Just because I made the smallest of errors about William and forgot he was coming. I talked about it with him last week. He asked me when the fireworks order was being delivered, and one thing led to another, and I suggested today. You can hardly blame me – we agreed to keep everything business as usual right up to the last. Like I said, I wanted to find a way to give him a tip. Of course, it slipped my mind last night that he was coming. I mean what is October without us ordering fireworks?"

Beatrix looked at Dora's hands – they were trembling. Realising that they were observed, Dora moved them to the brooch at the neck of her frock and fiddled with the pin as if checking it were not loose.

"Am I right to think something is up with our plan?" Beatrix asked, hoping against hope that she didn't already know the answer.

"It is and nothing you say now will change me. Upstairs . . . just now . . . I made up my mind. I don't want us to . . . to . . . do the thing we have talked about doing for so long. Tonight. The thing we talked about again yesterday before I went up to bed – to break the law and take our own lives. I just can't go through with it. I'm sorry Beattie."

"I thought as much. Don't be sorry, but don't make this a thing that only I wanted to do, or imagine the dreaded sickening fear of doing it is only on your side."

"Believe me when I say I want to be dead and floating

19

above it all, looking down on those bastards as they feel all the things they should feel ... all the guilt Terry should feel ... all the guilt some folk in this small-minded village should feel ... but I can't do it myself."

"Dora, we have talked and talked till we are blue in the face. We have both circled and circled and evaded and played things endlessly down the line, but we have run out of road. You do understand what is next don't you? I can't protect us anymore. I have fought this off for nearly two years now ... grizzly, begging meetings at the bank, the warning letters from Terry about the rent, the drip, drip of time wasting away with no business and no options but to stand our ground and stretch things out. But when the bailiffs come tomorrow ... and they are coming, have no doubt ... we are to be shamed and the whole village will know our business. We are homeless ... we are bankrupted."

"I know all that, but I just can't take my life, end my life, even with you at my side doing the same thing ... together ... however bleak the future. Even with the gentle slide-out route of the clever old sleeping pills and the gas fire. I've said this before, and I am saying it now, and I mean it. I can't do it, Beattie. I am so sorry."

"Oh, do stop fiddling with that dammed brooch Dora!" Beatrix took the trembling hands in hers. "I am truly sorry, but the game is up, old girl."

"I know that perfectly well," said Dora, fat tears sliding down her cheeks, though she was clearly doing her best not to cry.

Beatrix wondered what was coming next, for she knew Dora so well something decidedly was; she gave Dora her handkerchief and let the silence hang, forcing whatever it was out into the open.

At last Dora spoke. "I know you won't ask for fear of a point-blank refusal ... but might Alice and Harold take us in, if you called her ... if you begged?"

"Darling heart, I think you have gone mad." So, this was it. Dora was clutching at previously abandoned straws.

"Please Beattie, just try it? What if you explained, told her the truth? For God's sake she's your sister. She must, in her heart of hearts, know about us. Tell her the truth, please? Please think about it again, Beattie. Think about telling her? Please? Let me come with you? I can't face Wycombe House with its blank-faced, toothless old crones and bedclothes that smell of someone else's wee." The voice was rising in pitch, the heart palpating, Beatrix knew the signs. Dora's weak nerves and threatened blackouts had lived with them day in and day out these forty years. Despite herself she began to run round the old circular track one more time.

"Yes, I do refuse to ask my sister if we can live all cosy in her back-to-back because I know what Harold will say. And what would that life be like I ask you – even if she agreed and defied her husband – because I begged her? Sat every morning in their tiny kitchen looking at our hands, sat every evening in the small front room with nothing to say?"

"Well, that is what you will be doing if you go there on your own, Beattie. And I go to the poorhouse."

"They don't have poorhouses any more Dora, you know that. Stop being melodramatic."

"Well, they might as well be from what I hear and I am not doing this for effect." said Dora, her voice rising with the pressure of fighting back.

"OK. OK." Beatrix knew she had to be careful. Too much pushback from her now and Dora would take to her bed. "That's precisely why I am not going to let us end up homeless. Why ... if I can damn well help it ... you are not going into a home."

"But if we don't go to Durham what is to happen? We've no money to speak of. Our post office savings are gone, and the state pension isn't enough to cover any rent as well as our food ..." Dora was slipping back into the panic that had returned them countless times to the terrible conclusion they had already made; better dead than separate. Better break the law and take the suicide exit route. Better dead than life with her sister Alice, and Dora in Wycombe House.

"I don't know." Beatrix sat back in her chair; she felt totally drained. Nothing was resolved when last night she had thought that it finally was. Or had she? Perhaps it was just her hope that it was. What had she become if Dora was right? Perhaps she was guilty of cajoling and manipulating? How unforgivable if that had been the case ... It made her hate herself even more. How disgusting. She truly thought it had been clear and resolved between them and that was why she wrote to Oliver.

"It's my fault you know, for living too long."

"Please Dora if you can't say something sensible, don't say anything at all. We have both outlived our small inheritances if that is what you mean."

"Or rather, spent them, trying to survive in this damn place," said Dora, ruefully.

"Well what other option did we have?" Beatrix looked down at her hands resting again on the oilcloth, the cloth she wiped at least three times a day, seven days a week. Her hands looked dry and gnarled, the veins passing over each other just under her skin; from younger threads they had thickened to lumpy string – yet still so full of purpose. Who was she to stop that flow? She looked down at Dora's hands, whose liver spots looked like kisses of brown lipstick. Why should she expect someone who was forced as a child to ignore her left hand and only use her weaker right to be able to have a firm grip on things? Why should she expect someone who had lived her life in a directionless wriggling squiggle to turn herself into a lover of sticking to a straight line?

"What are you thinking?" Dora asked, handing back the handkerchief.

"I have no idea," Beatrix said, quietly, exhausted by the burden of it all. They listened as the kettle became increasingly agitated, its hot bottom jumping on the stove.

"Why don't you get some air, Beattie? Go and see to the hens. I will have my breakfast and open up. Take some time? Please?"

"I think I will."

"Will you telephone? Cancel Oliver? Or go for a walk with him as usual?" Dora asked.

"I haven't decided what to do for the best yet," Beatrix said, quickly. Why should she come up with the answers that might put back together something that Dora had unravelled? She already knew she would have to meet Oliver for their Thursday afternoon walk as usual, explain about the letter. Unless ... the clock said just before half past seven ... she could go out the back door as if to the hens and dash to the front down the side path. She might just catch Fred – catch him emptying his post box. Do something to stop time.

"What did you say to William by the way?" Dora called, as Beatrix left the room.

"I gave him a sixpence out of your till ..."

"Well then, you are just as bad as me!" called Dora, laughing.

Chapter Two

Beatrix pulled on what Dora sarcastically called her hen hat and coat and was quickly out of the back door and left onto the narrow path that ran down the side of the house. She unlatched the side gate, her fingers moving fast, out onto the pavement. She headed to the red post box. The metal tab announced 11am. Fred and the half past seven collection had just gone. She looked up and down the road; not a sign of him. She went to the front door, bent down, and looked through the open mouth of their letterbox, careful not to make too much noise in the movement and attract Dora's attention. She could see two brown envelopes, more bills, on the mat. That confirmed it. He had come and her letter was on its way to Oliver, to arrive first thing tomorrow morning. Damn it. She looked back down the road hoping to conjure up the postman in the far distance. The mist was lifting, and the dawn was breaking over the hill beyond the field at the back of the house. A Morris Minor car with its lights dimmed swept past. She walked slowly back through the side gate, back into a world where nothing could ever be put right. What to do? What a mess. This was the last day in this place – but, if to leave this life was no longer an option, then where on earth were they heading?

She went out the back and switched on the overhead light to the lean-to wash-house and tipped the pots of concentrated night-time amber-coloured wee down the loo. She pulled the long chain three times; the cistern clanked away, adjusting to the influx of fresh water. When they moved here, they had begged the GPO, their landlord then, to let them have the wash-house upgraded and replace the cupboard-sized lavvie at the end of the garden with its primitive soak away. Before this innovation, bathing had been old-style in the scullery, in front of the warming stove, in the tin bath that widowed Mrs Henderson had left behind, along with the ghost of her young marriage. The privacy was a boon at first from their bed-sit life in the Cromwell Road, no more traipsing up and down the corridor with your washbag and towel in your dressing gown and slippers clutching a wad of Izal to the shared lavvie, no more trying to ignore the aggressive jiggling of the latch on the bathroom door to say your fifteen minutes bathing time was up. Yet, they both grew to resent this basic set up just as bitterly, regarding it in time as a comedown from the chilly London bathroom with its stubborn gas geyser that they had retrospectively become fond of.

After the initial installation of a bathtub and loo innovation had not touched the wash-house with its old mangle awaiting the weekly clothes wash. The sink provided a single cold tap and the thin-metal tub, that at least had a plug hole, still needed to be filled by the kettle from the stove. These meagre up-grades, installed by a local lad a few years after they moved here, all looked so careworn and old-fashioned now compared to the spanking new bathrooms and twin-tubs she saw being installed into the village houses these days. Not the Cromwell Road white cast-iron round-bellied baths with feet, but in the modern style: huge porcelain lozenges of salmon pink, or lime green, like the ones in the magazines Dora loved to point out with matching sinks and loos, complete with discreet built-in cisterns.

The joys of a bath were now lost to Dora; she said for fear of slipping, but in truth she gave it up years before her mobility was reduced to its current low point, for fear of the wash-house's spidery corners, and from time to time the resident toad that crept under the door from the coal-bunker opposite and gave her the willies. Beatrix still used it to bathe once a week and wash her hair, whereas Dora plumped for a daily stand up wipe down, plus a shampoo and set at Avril's in the village once a fortnight. Sometimes Beatrix would take her time over a long soak, lying back and reading a novel borrowed from Oliver, the dampening pages weakly illuminated by the single overhead lamp, or leave it switched off and light up some of the waxed paper-wrapped tea lights that rested on the rim of the bath and float free, the warmth of all that carefully heated water easing her tired back.

Beatrix stepped out of the wash-house and turned right, down the path to the garden. The horizon had turned a rich red as the sun's rays pierced a bleeding sky. The ploughed fields at this distance looked soft as demerarea sugar; the rising sun turning the usual patchwork of recently ploughed brown soil to golden. She pulled open the door to her potting shed which leaned against the left-hand garden wall. Though not at all keen on her running a sweet shop, her father appreciated the idea of a kitchen garden and had given her a complete set of tools when they moved in. She had a wall frame made, just like his, on which they were set out in military order. In her childhood she would follow him round as he worked in his garden, and he, loving her company, would show her all the tricks; how to oil and sharpen the tools, how to mend them and keep them ready for action; *A good gardener keeps his kit tidy.*

Despite her deep affection for this garden now, it had not been Beatrix's heart's desire to come here. In the depths of the Great War, she had frequently passed by enticing adverts for roles for women on her work noticeboard at the bank. Yet one caught her eye, and she kept returning to it – a postmistress position and the free GPO house tenancy that went with it. She only mentioned it to Dora in passing, in the belief that the thought of leaving London and all that went with it was beyond her comprehension. Dora, however, had seen an article in *The Lady* and, being easily influenced, it had encouraged her to feel romantically positive about a lifestyle Dora had never once encountered in any true sense since her childhood, but one that appeased all her war-jangled aspirations – country air.

Dora had convinced herself that a woman, born in Paris, so naturally with a free-thinking, egalitarian outlook on life – though in truth brought up from the age of six by her teacher parents with her little sister in Balham – was wasted living in a bedsit in the Cromwell Road, teaching French on an occasional basis to private pupils. Here, in the country, Dora could, she was sure, find her *métier*, supporting Beatrix to run a village post office and living a life breathing clean, peaceful air. A little village, conveniently not that far away from London and its weekend nightlife that they could still enjoy. So much so that when they came down on the train to High Wycombe, caught the bus and stood outside, it was only Beatrix who felt apprehension. Dora encouraged her to stand here in this spot and see the potential, see how Beatrix could feed them both from the garden and live well from the proceeds of her income as a post mistress, find security and a purpose. A community indeed, but out here, as Dora came to learn and Beatrix's more cautious instinct feared, it mattered far more how you lived, than what you did for a living.

As for the fresh air, this form of countryside was nothing like County Durham. *Suburban* Beatrix's father would have called it with a sneer. It was a fantasy that this would be a welcoming place, with a community of kindred spirits who would turn a kindly blind eye, or perhaps even welcome their set-up. Almost from the off there was a nose in the air and an obvious whisper behind the hand. Neither of them was interested in the church, so that was no help; nor were they welcomed at the Women's Institute – not that either would have gone, but the lack of an invitation rankled Dora the most; it hurt, it hurt. Though they stuck at it through a lack of alternatives, suburbia it turned out was not their *milieu* after all.

She breathed in the air in the potting shed. The particular mix of compost, linseed oil and turps, kept a few degrees warmer than the outside, was to her one of the most delicious smells in the entire world; it grounded her. This was the place where she made new life grow, where her seeds and cuttings were germinated and pricked out, where her bulbs were brought to rest and sleep out their time waiting to be replanted in the autumn, and the place where a dozen seven-day old chicks were kept warm every spring by a paraffin heater with a water trough at its base. She bought them from Mr Greengage's farm down the road, having once in her first innocent year bought fertilised eggs. She hadn't fully comprehended the pressures of keeping the eggs in an incubator, watching them hatch, throwing away the failed ones and drowning the boys at a few days old. She had submerged them one by one under the water feeling their tiny beating hearts slow to a stop in the palm of her hand; one hand holding down her own resistant wrist, deep in the bucket for far longer than was strictly necessary, but she could not bear the idea that they might come out struggling to live, only to die in her hand gasping for air. Buying pre-sexed chicks was by far the better way. She could sit, guilt-free, with the lucky tiny fluffy yellow girls for a short while every day, watching them scuttle as she threw them thin shreds of baby lettuce fresh from the cold frame. Dora hated the hens, too unpredictable and flighty. Beatrix held them at an appropriate distance from her heart, never gave them names though she knew people who did that. How could you bring yourself to eat something that had once been called Enid or Evie, Millicent or Mo?

At the end of the shed was the metal bin that held the seed for the hen feed. She knocked twice on the side from a fear of mice, or worse, rats, and plunged the long cylindrical shovel into the pile. The mix of seed slipped down the metal slope and from there into her bucket; one scoop per hen. She had forgotten the scraps from last night that were in a bowl by the stove – hardly surprising with a mind full of such confusion, but no matter she would return later; it would be a good excuse to get more air. Out here the natural rhythms had always taken over, if she let them; out here life went on – away from the prying eyes of the village.

She carried on down the path. The copse of trees appeared untethered, floating on a sea of rising mist that had come to rest beneath the tip of the hill and the valley of ploughed earth below – a manifestation of the Elysian Fields perhaps? How lucky to be one of the souls floating there – the virtuous dead freed from care, all their hard decisions made, the moment of death past, now on their way. Down here in the land of the mortals the fight to stay alive went on.

How quickly the horizon changed; the flow of blood-light into the sky was staunched, the sun's complete arrival churning the horizon to yellow, deepening the blues above, hastening the night frost's retreat. Another dawn of another day. What could have convinced her that suicide was a realistic means of escape? She and not Dora was the fool for having thought they would ever be strong-willed enough. Why blame Dora? Beatrix had no idea if she could go through with it herself. Holding Dora fixed in the same mental space had taken all her attention and stopped her from facing up to the fact that it had been a ridiculous, overly dramatic, terrifying notion to take their lives, not feasible, not their way. Now that flawed plan was in the bin, she had to begin to create a new belief within herself that life would, in some as yet unimaginable way, go on. They would compromise and live with Alice in Durham – oh Lord, don't, just don't think about that, just look at that sky – or perhaps live separately, in a lonely life for sure, but a life. Hadn't that been what her father always said? *Don't fight girls, for the Lord's sake, compromise.*

The hens lived at the far end of the garden, beyond her fruit trees and vegetable patch, now all tucked up – cut back, turned, lifted, composted, set ready for next spring. The seed potatoes raised, the apples picked from the tree, the pear tree espaliered into submission like a surrendered soldier, arms spread-eagled against the wall as if to face the firing squad; everything shipshape. This year's clear-up hadn't been any more special or particular – this was how she always ran it. She hoped the new tenants would love it and keep it as she had after the Hendersons. It gave her pride to stand straight-legged, braced against uncertainty and look at all she had achieved. So much potential to come and her, the one alone, who had tended to it.

The world had so long to go, this garden so long to grow, millennia stretching ahead. As her Greek myths and legends schoolbooks taught her, Persephone would return here year on year from the underworld, the winter would end, the spring would come to this garden, even when it no longer belonged to Beatrix. The shop would be far better off without them in its life; she didn't have to die to let it go.

The hen house was set in a circle of dirt and surrounded by a high chicken wire fence, into which she had made a gate with a significant latch. The shed was raised above ground level by three old wooden beams that ran horizontally from side to side. It had three entrances and exits, the main runner up to the front door and a couple that led to small wooden shutters, one on either side. She often wondered how it must have felt for the dozen or so hens hunched and silent in the darkness, as they awaited the nightly attempt by the foxes to foil her lock in. Sensing, more than hearing movement, she imagined the hens bracing as the foxes sniffed and circled the fence around the little wooden shack, trying every so often to dig under the chicken wire, break through from underneath the floorboards and poke their foxy faces up into the middle of a room full of startled eyes. Though the chicken wire was folded and buried deep into the ground it was her weekly task to repair the fresh holes dug around the perimeter. It formed a weak first-line deterrent for the foxes as breaching the hen house itself presented them with a further major challenge – but she wanted to make them have to work hard. Did the hens remain silent, heads under wings, breathing quietly, praying? Were some nesting boxes regarded as safer than others inside? A better nesting box on the upper levels and further from the door? A darker corner? The early bird to bed making a selection based on a pure hunch. Twice in the early days the foxes had got in and killed them all. A few more times, before she got better at the game, she came out here too late in the afternoon to find a traumatised flock missing a couple of companions pulled through a small hole in the fence. In the second war she had equated her battle against the foxes with the ebb and flow of the battles against the Hun. As the positive news vacillated so she renewed her battlements. A satisfying fight for supremacy between a lone *Homo Sapiens* and a score of voracious *Vulpes*.

Beatrix climbed the wooden runner and raised the main shutter. Out they scuttled, clucking, scratching, and flapping their pathetic wings.

"Here chick chick ... here chuck chuck ..." and she flung handfuls of seed wide and high as they nipped about, their twitching toes scrabbling to keep up with the dance conducted by her swinging arms. She checked their water trough and ran the tap a bit to top it up – though it hardly needed it. She went to either side of the shed and raised the side shutters – one of the more stupid of the hens poked its head out and looked down, as if the little jump required were a terrifying prospect.

"Well, if you won't use the front door then these are the consequences you stupid, stupid bird."

Tipping out the last of the seed from the pail she collected the broom from its place by the door and stepped back up the runner, which sprung up and down a little under her weight. She used the broom and pail like a circus performer with props to steady her and stooped to get through the doorway, created by the raised shutter. Remaining hunched due to the low roof, she took pleasure in gently sweeping out the anxious feathery arse that was poking half in and half out of the shutter hole; it disappeared with a raucous splutter of indignity that made her smile.

At the far end of the hen house were two rows of ten nesting boxes. She had cleared out and re-laid these with straw the day before, so they remained clean enough. The floor though could do with a sweep out to clear the night's excretions. Whatever tomorrow might bring she wanted it shipshape, she wanted it properly done. She took some clean straw from the bale in the corner and scattered it about and added some to the bottom of her metal pail.

Looking in the top row of nests there were two eggs in one and one single in another. Nothing was more delightful than the feel of an egg in its nest. Her cold hand reached out to hold the blood-warm egg that rolled so willingly into her palm. Held within that perfect shape – defined in its laying – was the hope of birth and succession. She had talked with Oliver on one of their walks about her thoughts on this and he told her his understanding of the Hindu view of the cow and why it is sacred. He explained that the existence of a cow in the family provides the opportunity for ongoing life; its excrement fuel, its power given to the plough, its milk nourishment, its offspring the confirmation of sustaining a future and, in death, its hide clothing. It made her look at her hens afresh and appreciate the symbi-otic nature of their relationship. What was the purpose of a hen if not to feed you and confirm the eternal circularity of life without beginning or end?

Which came first? Her father's tease knew full well the conundrum was wasted on his sure-minded elder daughter. Beatrix did not allow herself the luxury of time-wasting shadows of doubt on her view. The hen. She picked up a long orange feather and put it in her hat; it used to have two small green and purple feathers in its ribbon, which went west a long time ago. She smiled; this would confirm to the village that she was definitely losing her marbles. Four more eggs from the lower deck joined the three in the bottom of the cold pail – beginning their transition from future life force to supper.

As she retreated backwards down the plank with her trophies, Beatrix was surprised to see the horse walking purposefully towards her across the nearby field. Not with his head held high, but almost parallel to his body, his long neck reaching forward as if smelling her in the air more than seeing her. His large hooves, the ends of his great fore and back legs, plodded the sticky turf to greet her. She put down her pail with its cooling eggs and walked to the fence – the sunlight now so bright she had to shield her eyes to properly see him. He stopped a few paces back from the fence, his head raised in expectation.

"Good morning. I am very sorry indeed, but I have nothing for you today. Nothing at all, poor old boy."

He snorted hard, his lungs warming the air between them and stepped forward, nodding his head up and down. *Come on now*, he seemed to gesture, *time to hand over the goods*; utilising his telepathic powers to convey what was required through the generosity of his approach. His chestnut coat was rough on his haunches, yet silky smooth on his back, the nap of his coat defined his spine from his shoulders to his tail, which needed a good clean with a wire brush. His mane was impressive; his large head must weigh a ton. She reached out her hand to stroke his forehead and he stepped back.

"You see . . . I didn't know you were coming old lad."

The horse stood looking at her – his eyes moved past her

to the hens pecking and cooing like old women exchanging gossip at the market. He lifted his head up and down. If he would dare go closer, he would be nudging her, pushing her to *go-get-the thing*.

"I know – I am a stupid woman – why don't I get it?" Beatrix walked over to where her apple trees stood with empty arms. She looked about her on the ground and there was a rotten half of an ancient apple – fly-blown and boozy. She took it to the horse and offered it up on her flat hand as an apology. He approached, *at last the woman got the deal*, and his ginger whiskery lips felt their way over the offering that didn't amount to much and took it, nonetheless, moving it round his mouth, making light work of the decomposing mush.

"What must it sound like in your head – the noise of your eating is so loud out here – I can't imagine." And she put her hand out again to the white blaze that drew her, and he stood still enough to let her stroke his now patient face.

His neck was warm, warming her hands as they slid down the waxy hair on his throat and over to his mane, which was rougher to the touch than it looked. He felt glorious, powerful, a friend – yet only when it pleased him. Many times, she had stood at this fence, and he had stared at her from a great distance as she called to him – only to return to eating grass, having no desire for her company.

Whatever his past rejection she was grateful to him for his need of her today. Though Beatrix had only ridden the beach donkeys at Scarborough she had watched the passing horse riders in the lanes here with fascination; she despised the hunt and all that went with it, ghastly people, ghastly business, yet she could imagine the feeling of companionship and mutual pleasure in roaming and running wild together that a horse must provide. How much she loved those donkeys. Round and round she would go till her mother and father, him in his suit and tie, her full-bellied and in her Sunday dress, would slope off to the deck chairs without her. They didn't return for years after Alice was born – their father sinking so far into his grief at the loss of his wife that he had little thought for his children and what good a holiday might do for them all. By the time, at her begging, he took them back, Alice was six and Beatrix, now aged twelve, had become too big to ride the little beasts. Having encouraged Alice across the beach for a ride she'd hung around watching the donkeys for so long that her father would return from his lonely stroll and drift off with Alice down to the water's edge without her. Eventually the donkey man took pity and would let her lead a donkey with a small child on its back round the track marked out with little flags on sticks in the sand, whilst he took the money from the punters. She had loved it and soon it became her seasonal role, running across the fine sand to be greeted by the man on the first day of their annual holiday – *here's my little helper back again* he would laugh, and they would slip back into the routine. Only one hour she was allowed of it though – Alice and their father would arrive and then it was time to be off and away back to being father's little helper – mother to Alice.

She could feel Alice's sweet-sticky face right in her own, her warm breath blasting out wine gum fumes, as they lay on the hot beach at the line where the high tide met the edge of the dry sand, waiting for their father to finish his swim and come and fetch them; for Alice to play in the shallows and for Beatrix to endure her dreaded swimming lesson.

Ta ra . . . ta ra!
Get out of my face Alice.

Ta ra! Ta ra! D'you like my new way of saying goodbye Beattie? Tonks taught it me.

Tonks taught it TO me. Tonks is not really the best teacher you know.

You just don't like him coz he lives in a small house and his mother works for us. He is, he is my best friend, and he knows waaaay more than you.

Hmm. Alice, try this – screw up your eyes and look at the sky. Goes all purple at the edges – see.

Father says you shouldn't do that you'll go blind.

Not at the sun silly – the sky. See– it goes purple at the horizon, that's a prism, at least I think that is what it is.

Don't be stupid . . . what prison is in the sky?

A mother to Alice – what a sham notion that had been. Patients in and out of the drawing room that doubled as a surgery, hour after hour, on top of long absences on his rounds trudging the back-to-backs in the mining villages, listening to the wheezing chests of Durham miners. His absence pushed them all to sacrifice for the greater good, but she was never maternal and Alice never an accepting child. The moment Alice could fend for herself Beatrix left all that caring. *Father there's a sick man at the door, I mean a gentleman, come to see you . . .* left for London as fast as she could at eighteen, didn't she. After all he had Alice – they had each other, didn't they – and she never for a moment considered returning.

Beatrix breathed in the rancid, sweaty, pure smell of the horse. As she stroked its neck her mind returned to her conundrums. She would have to carefully manage the tricky matter of Oliver and the letter. Had she been deceiving herself? She was certain when she posted it that Dora agreed that this afternoon, they would leave the world behind. Hadn't they gone over the arrangements again last night before Dora tottered up to bed? Beatrix was to telephone Oliver this morning and say she wasn't well – a headache – so their regular walk was cancelled. They would shut the shop at one o'clock for early closing, as normal on a Thursday. No need for shocks or surprises, no customers knocking on the door. Swallow down Dora's many hoarded sleeping pills with warm milk and sugar, roll the towels along the door sill, switch on – but not light – the gas fire in the bedroom, lie down on the bed, hold hands and drift away – a final act of illegal defiance. Done. She had determined a while back that she would write to Oliver to explain everything, ask him to manage their affairs, tidy it all up and contain – if such a thing were possible – the gossip, hold on to their truth. It was planned that Oliver would get the letter in the morning and come. She had hoped he would be the one to find them first. He would know what to do. He would honour the way they had chosen to die and know why; he, above all others, would understand in a heartbeat once he knew everything. He would protect their memory, sort out the hens, phone Alice, arrange the funeral and he would do it – perfectly.

Last night, when she had finished the letter and come to bed, Dora was already out for the count under the eiderdown, snuffling. Beatrix had wanted a moment before sleeping – to hold hands and acknowledge the enormity of the night ahead and the day to come. Finding Dora so deeply asleep had left her alone with her thoughts, but not with any fear. Fear was in the unknown of the life ahead, the certainty of death a release. Now she understood, the sleeping pills had been a deliberate ploy by Dora – knocking herself out before the big day; the big day when Dora dumped the plan. Despite her disappointment – was it truly disappointment, how could that be – she didn't blame Dora, she admired her. Beatrix shouldn't cancel Oliver, she should honour their routine of a Thursday walk, she owed him that and explain, somehow explain, that when the letter arrived tomorrow, he should rip it up unread. He was an honourable man; he would, she was sure, do as she asked of him. She would tell him of their troubles and reassure him that there was no drama now, but a new plan in which they would face the bailiffs and then leave – as long as she could square things with Alice – for Durham.

The horse had enough of her absent-minded stroking. He pushed her arm away with his head and backed off before turning and trotting into the field, shaking the stroke of her hand from his twitching neck. She would have to go back in the house and, sooner rather than later, she would have to phone Alice.

"That's right you shrug me off, see if I care," she said, voicing the rejection as if she were talking to Alice, with a vehemence that can only be used to berate a younger sister and cause no offence; "Ta ra horse and ta ra hens!" Beatrix said, picking up the pail of eggs and walking up the garden path, and in through the back door.

She took off her hen hat, turning the cloche in her hand, its patchy dark green velvet now complemented by a hen feather. It was a fair enough jibe of Dora's; Beatrix did have a highly frugal disposition. She'd had to. Items, originally bought for going up to town, progressed through stages until in their final incarnation they were for the hens and the garden. She had fallen in love with the matching coat and hat shopping in Regent Street on one of their first trips up to London from here. She felt the thin coat lapel between her fingers. A workhorse of a garment that had suited her in her forties, it had been shortened over time and had many a new button; you could say something for a Dickins & Jones outfit – it lasted. She had come cautiously out of the changing room to get Dora's approval.

Oh Beattie, that look will take you to a lot of places!
Well yes, and no.

Chapter Three

The tea remained warm in the brown pot and her breakfast place laid, complete with her silver napkin ring. The
matching pair were twenty-first birthday gifts from Dora's
mother; Beatrix's ring was intended for a husband that had
been encouraged to be looked for, in increasingly anxious
letters written in the French of her mother's tongue. The
clock ticked; all was as it should be. She looked through
the scullery doorway into the shop and saw Dora tottering
across in her heels to raise the blind, flip the sign to 'open'
and lift the snib on the latch to unlock the door.

"I'm back," Beatrix called over her shoulder as she set the
pail with its seven eggs on the draining board. She would
let them rest here before joining the others on the slate in
the pantry.

"Righto. You have some breakfast," Dora replied, grabbing the local paper from the stand before working her way,
hand over hand, back around her counter and sinking down
onto the stool, a deflating silken balloon. Dora loved the
local paper – its gossip and its puzzles filled the interludes
between the customers, as the predictable day rolled by.
Through its pages she vicariously joined in with the activi-
ties her snobbish disposition never could have allowed her to

enjoy – the Easter egg hunt winners, the flower and produce show squabbles, the bring and buy recipe wars and the poor show at the fundraising tea dance for the crumbling church. From her throne behind her counter, Dora chit chatted the day away with her few remaining customers – fed by the highly questionable journalism she found in the *Bucks Free Press*.

Beatrix put a slice of bread on the hot plate and lowered the lid. She warmed her hands. They were always cold, nothing she could do, weak circulation. Cold hands and cold feet – Dora's constant moan when, at last, she slid into bed beside her. She flipped the slice and glanced at the clock; Dora was opening up bang on eight, from the outside they appeared back on track. She took her tea and toast to the table. If someone wanted anything from her side of the business – the shreds of her post office mistress role that remained – then Dora could summon her, and she would go on parade. She needed time to *get her face straight* as Dora would say. Better to stay for a bit longer *out back and not out front* – as Dora would also say. A *bon mot* she pinched from one of her theatrical crowd; found at the Gateways club, Dora would flirt with them wildly, then lure them into her circle of friends, after which she could become a keen camp follower, faithfully traipsing round back stage, show after show. Would they have been happier continuing in London – rather than becoming the regular weekend visitors they grew to be before the Blitz scared them off? Would staying in the Cromwell Road have been better than here? Her clinging on at the bank if she were lucky and Dora continuing her private French lessons to the handful of School Certificate failures and down on their luck debutants who climbed the stairs to the little bedsit with heavy hearts, having ignored their present and imperfect conjugations since the lesson the previous week. It was hard to say, the world of difference between London and the sticks was palpable. Out here, as Dora discovered to her chagrin, no one wanted to learn French – not after we saved them twice from the Germans. London was a freer associating ragbag of people, some of whom washed up into their shared housing, which was converted from a huge pile at an optimistic time just before the Great War. It comprised of a few bed-sitting rooms of various sizes from the much-coveted ex-reception rooms on the ground floor upwards; the residents, mostly young working women, a few elderly biddies and the odd (sometimes very odd) single gent. Their room was at the back on the first floor, so very well placed for them to hold their own in the pecking order of the house hierarchy. It was spacious enough; they had a gas fire as well as a geyser for hot water and a primus stove on which they cooked. They could relax at the end of the day in a couple of ropy old comfy chairs that Alice had given up as moth-eaten in her view.. They had to leave them behind when they moved down here, the small sit-ting room being converted into the shop meant there was no room for armchairs, though they had managed to bring the little wooden table at which they sat and ate in London and now did the same in the scullery. The best place of all was the large back garden which their bed-sit overlooked, which Beatrix, along with a couple of other female tenants, gradually reclaimed. In retrospect it had been the perfect place to be two co-habiting women, one in their early twenties and one in their early thirties. If any one cared, and most people didn't, she was the younger friend helping an older spinster out by sharing accommodation. Two single beds lying quietly behind a decoupage dressing screen said all that was needed to be said.

There was the theatre, there were dances with no issue about women dancing together with so many men absent at the front. She had her wage to sustain them in all the basics and Dora's pin money added some flair to their lives, but, as the top brass at the bank began to make clear, they were focused on supporting the returning men. She had watched as the pool of pinafore-wearing female clerks was subsumed by the flood of their returning walking-wounded male counterparts; she had been wise to move on in '17 – rather than stay and count the days till her turn came. Life in a bed-sit began to feel tenuous, the war endless and the need to support the war effort compulsive. If she was honest the article in *The Lady* not only attracted Dora – it offered a way forward for herself, a way also to put back, to be purposeful, no better, counted. Lord only knows what the rent for that cramped bed-sit would be nowadays. Having watched as the old women crawled up the staircase, their bones creaking with the pain, banished to the very top of the building where the rents were cheapest, they both knew in their heart of hearts that way of living was a younger person's game.

She looked up at the clock again. The morning that started in such a rush now seemed to be moving in slow motion; she could hear the coo of the pigeons on the wash-house roof, she could feel her own pulse. What was it Peter Pan said? It leaped from the stage and into her heart on what was almost their first proper date. *To die would be an awfully big adventure.* They had been shocked at Barrie's lack of thought in putting such positive notions on death into the minds of the hundreds of younger hearts, whose eager faces were all around them in the Upper Circle. Later she had read that it was quite deliberate on his part, revealing, she felt, an unhealthy mental state, but she had come to fear Barrie was right. Life's options for adventure had reduced to a binary choice – dead, or alive and separated, and with Dora who knew where. She had been released from the bare-faced truth of that when she was outside, now back here at the kitchen table she felt sucked back into despair by the pressure of trying to live in the limbo between two unbearable options. That was how she had spent the night; awake as Dora slept – convincing herself she could do it with the help of Dora's pills. Well, them – and the gas.

"Even if we don't provide any fireworks, there's going to be the usual display on the green this November the 5th – let's hope they will use our local self-pronounced chief landlord and chief village cretin – Terry Longhurst – as the guy," called Dora, from her perch. "Perhaps he's too damp and sweaty to catch light? Though his layers of fat and oily personality would certainly sizzle nicely once the flames got a grip. His porkpie hat would make a particularly good moment don't you know. It would go up a treat into the sky ... whoosh. Once cooked they could slice him and sell him at Lyons Corner House – Terry *à la mode!*"

"Thanks for the breakfast and especially the cuppa!" Beatrix called back. "*Pure nectar from the Gods,* as my Dad would say. Did you have some?"

"Nah. Tummy's a bit dyspeptic – so I gave it a miss. Think it was the extra pill ... that will serve me. Mind you that toast smells very appetising, I will have something in a bit." There was a pause as Dora continued her reading. "I say, look at this. There's an obituary for Winifred Thompson in the paper. Do you remember her? She was a friend of that girl Betty, who lived in the room opposite on our floor in Cromwell Road – you know the one who gave us the leaflets for the Women's Sunday in Hyde Park in '07 and sucked us into the National Union of Women's Suffrage lot? Well, she's dead."

"Betty?"

"No, do keep up dear – Winifred Thompson. There's an obit for her. Turns out she was born and brought up here and came back to live in Penn in her sixties. We never knew."

"I can't recall her at all, you have a much better memory for all those old girls."

"Yes, you will . . . you must do. Winifred was the one who got up at dawn with that Australian chanteuse that we went and saw at the Wigmore Hall – Muriel Mathers – on the day we were leafletting the Women's Sunday March. It tells the story in here of how they got themselves out to Hendon that same day and went and put Muriel into an airship, in order to drop thousands of our leaflets on Westminster – only Muriel got clean blown off course and ended up in Surrey, and up a tree, for the Lord's sake and I don't know what. Winifred was running about all over trying to follow Muriel's flight path in a cab. You must remember that story – Betty told us! Remember? There was a hell of a fuss at the time. There's even a photograph of Winifred standing next to the blessed airship before it took off with Muriel and her pilot – a man called Mr Spencer. I mean it took some pluck, didn't it? Doing something like that. She was even older than me – made it to '79 poor dear soul. Funny she washed up in this neck of the woods; I wish we'd have known her better then, because we could have found her out here. It would have been jolly."

"Makes you wonder who else we missed round about."

"Aye up, we are not alone . . ."

The doorbell jangled. Beatrix stood up, automatically

on duty, then stopped herself and sat back down to listen and wait.

"Ah now, good day-to-you, Miss Moyle!" Dora was in her element, playing it up for the scullery audience out back, with kiss-curled Miss Moyle as her stooge. Beatrix was glad she had kept Dora innocent of Terry's planned role for Miss Moyle and the key tomorrow morning, no need, what would come would come. This was Miss Moyle's regular visit to collect her weekly romance magazine on a Thursday before catching the bus to High Wycombe, to make the tea and sort the filing at Terry Longhurst's Estate Agency. She didn't actually sell the houses, but that did not matter one jot to Dora, house buying and selling was a rich gossipy seam to mine. Relations had remained cordial with Miss Moyle despite their growing animosity to her boss.

"Good day, Miss Ham," said Miss Moyle. "Is Miss Veal's counter not open? I am wanting some note cards."

"No, not to worry at all. Though I could serve you, of course, I think Miss Veal is in earshot. Miss Veal are you there by any chance? Miss Moyle requires the post office." Beatrix rose; moving her plate and its toast crumbs to the draining board, she smoothed down her skirt, set her face to meet the world, pushed herself out of the scullery and into the shop.

"Miss Moyle! How can I help you?"

"I noticed the other week you had some lovely note cards with wildflowers on them. Am I right?" said the fashionable young woman, all perfect lipstick and straight stockings, her twenty-two years spent in certain hope of love – the same age as Beatrix when she moved in with Dora.

"These? Or these? Or perhaps these?" Beatrix laid out the cards on the counter and added the last two from her unseen miserly stock underneath.

"Goodness me what a treasure trove you have under there, these are lovely. How much?"

"One penny each. Now I come to think of it, they are running down this particular line, so you can have two for the price of one," said Beatrix, taking an altogether opposite stance from her usual penny-pinching ways and visibly surprising Miss Moyle as a result, who now stared at her with her big blue eyes.

"I say, that is a lucky break. I will have this one with the buttercups and . . . I think . . . yes, this with the dear pansies. And oh, I nearly forgot my mag!" Miss Moyle turned, her hemline following her slip just a second later, as Beatrix watched in admiration of the girl's carefully curated allure, aware Dora would be doing the same. She slid her weekly pleasure onto the counter – a man and a woman in an embrace, her leaning back in twin-set and pearls, him in Brylcreem and all-powerful. Beatrix found a paper bag and unlocked her cash tin. She looked at Miss Moyle's hands – her red-tipped nails, plump little strawberries, dipped into her purse and produced the coins.

"Perhaps a small bag of dolly mixtures or some humbugs on your ration?" Dora was clearly in a competitive mood for Miss Moyle's attention.

"No thanks, my keep fit group at the WI would never allow it," said Miss Moyle, looking genuinely sad.

"Dear me, dear, you don't want to listen to those bitter women – they suck all the pleasure out of the world, don't they Miss Veal? Somebody told me that you've sold the big house in Church Lane at last. Do tell. Will it be a very large family? I hope so."

"Yes, well sort of. Deal was done with Mr Longhurst this week. I believe it's going to be an hotel. It's a relief I can tell you. These huge old places are not wanted by hardly anyone anymore . . . way too much work to keep them up to scratch and absolutely no mod cons. We were getting worried it would have to be demolished like some."

"No mod cons? Sounds like this old place!" laughed Dora.

"Oh, not at all! Mr Longhurst says this little place will be snapped up in a jiffy. I mean not as a shop of course, but that could be easily rectified with everything ripped out in here and all modern appliances put in and sold for a good amount and quick, I'll be bound."

"I'll be bound," said Beatrix under her breath, whilst giving Miss Moyle her change and closing her cash box; any remaining goodwill to Miss Moyle was evaporating fast.

"I'll be bound, dear . . . suit Terry Longhurst to a tee . . ." said Dora, letting it hang.

"I am sorry that you are leaving, of course I am. The place won't be the same without this shop, but I suppose in the end it's progress . . . in a way. Where is it that you will be going?"

"A long way from here," said Beatrix.

"Well, that is a shame, so we won't be seeing you around?"

"By the way . . . will you be voting next week?" Beatrix couldn't resist it.

"Sorry?" said Miss Moyle, putting her purse back in her handbag.

"In the election?"

Dora gave her the look.

"Is there one? Really? My goodness, haven't we just had one?" said Miss Moyle looking uncomfortable.

"Yes. They say that Churchill will win it back off Attlee." Beatrix could feel Dora shifting off her stool.

"Well, though I honestly don't pay much attention, perhaps he should."

"I'm not sure. Miss Ham and I didn't march for the vote for women only to see an old drunk of a man running the country."

"Well, I never thought about it, but I mean, there isn't a woman standing is there? – or have I got that wrong?"

"No dear, you haven't," said Dora, trying to shut it down by sweeping imaginary icing sugar off her counter with the side of her hand – as if the sticky white dust was the topic of conversation that could be swept away.

"So ... you were suffragettes – how exiting that must have been. I bet you have some stories to tell ..."

"No, dear, we were suffragists," said Beatrix.

"Sorry, isn't that what I just said?

"Very near it. Don't let Miss Veal pull you back nearly fifty years into a debate over a fine distinction that was even lost on the participating women themselves. Some of them would do anything for a row, I used to say," said Dora.

"... And after all Churchill ... he won the war didn't he ...?" Miss Moyle looked to the paper bag holding her cards, held hostage on the counter by Beatrix's hand.

"That was six long years ago. He is older than time and as mad as a hatter. What is the point in having a democracy if people don't use their vote?" Beatrix could hardly claim to be surprised, but she found the ignorance, the foolishness, overly infuriating, though she knew it was her lack of ability to fight her real daemons that made her pick on the girl.

"Well, though he's far older, he's less potty than me, so that's a relief for us all!" said Dora, trying to rescue the moment, with a laugh.

"As I said, really pay no attention to me. I don't vote so I don't have a view. I think politics is so complicated that it's best to let it alone. Now I must catch my bus. Good morning, ladies!" and Miss Moyle grabbed her purchases from Beatrix's counter and fled.

"What on earth do you think you are you doing?" Dora said, half laughing, half furious. "Poor girl, she's too easy prey – and anyway you, of all people, getting into politics in the shop. IN THE SHOP? You are breaking your own bloody golden rules!"

"If Terry sends that imbecile here tomorrow to pick up the keys you had better deal with it. I really can't stand for it," said Beatrix, breaking her former resolve not to say anything and banging her hands on her counter. She was turning to go out back for some peace before the inevitable reaction from Dora, but before she could move far the doorbell bounced on its rocker and two schoolgirls in their school regalia sailed in.

"Well, good morning girls. On your way to school?" Dora was back in full sail, stating the bleeding obvious without caution, when Beatrix knew distinct caution was the name of the game with these two, based on previous experience. She turned back from the scullery door.

"I've got my ration coupon and a ha'penny. What's the most sweets I can get?" said Molly Clutterbuck. Her friend Mildred Winters giggled behind her. The girls looked as self-important as recently teenage schoolgirls so often do. The rules of their sect had laws of its own that covered everything from their looks to their language, to their manner, to their sniggering secrets.

"What can I get, PLEASE," Dora cooed at them. "Well now, let me see ..."

"I'll have as many of those gobstoppers as I can on the very top shelf behind you," said Molly, ignoring the correction.

Dora slid off her stool, dragged the stepladder level with

the shelves and clinging to the side rail, she tentatively climbed up beside the wall of dusty jars.

"Can I assist you?" Beatrix feared the total 'collapse of stout party' that would follow a slip.

"I'm perfectly able to cope, thank you."

The girls sniggered as Dora's behind lowered itself down the steps, her one arm clutching the jar, her other clinging to the rail. Just as she placed it on the counter Molly piped up.

"Actually, I've changed my mind. I want a bar of chocolate instead."

"Molly, you know perfectly well that we only sell loose sweets in this shop, and a few pleases and thank yous would not go amiss," said Beatrix, moving round from behind her counter.

"Give me the gobstoppers then," said a mutinous Molly.

"If you don't mind your manners, I may have to have a word with your mother the next time I see her," said Dora, as she placed a quarter of an ounce weight on the scales and counted the sweets onto the weighing machine with a set of tongs.

"No, you don't, you wouldn't dare upset her, she's just about your only customer left," said Molly.

"My Mum says no man would ever have looked at you twice. Why's that Miss Ham? Why's that?" Mildred Winters jumped up and down in the excitement of finally spitting out what she had so obviously been dared to say.

"I really couldn't say. I can't imagine why your mother would ever say such a thing," said Dora, dropping the paper cone of sweets down onto the counter.

Molly threw the ha'penny and her ration coupon on the floor, snatched the sweets, grabbed Mildred's hand, and fled.

The bell jangled slowly to a full stop.

Dora opened a jar of fudge and put two large lumps in her mouth at the same time. "I thought you said you felt dyspeptic this morning?" Beatrix moved slowly to pick up the discarded coin and the coupon.

"I'm trying a new method of appeasement," said Dora, with her mouth full. There was a long pause as the sticky goo slipped down her throat. "Ghastly those girls," she said with a final swallow.

"Yes, ghastly," agreed Beatrix, "just like being back at school."

"Just. I short-changed her, you know. She's minus one gobstopper on the deal." Dora winked.

"Perhaps you should have given her double rations and stopped her gob for good!"

Beatrix crossed over behind the sweet counter and gave Dora the coin and the coupon.

She hesitated for a second before placing her hand on Dora's face. An electric shock passed between the two. Thirty-four years of dissembling – of being shop-smart – wiped away by a forbidden gesture.

"Plenty of men and women looked at you with longing, but they never had a chance with me around."

Dora's button-brown eyes investigated Beatrix's grey-green ones and she smiled. "Sticks and stones. Sticks and stones, darling. All this pent-up bile against these people should have given you, as well as me, dyspepsia by now."

Beatrix looked down at Dora's hand resting on her arm. "I'm sorry Dora. I was the one who started the whole idea of coming here and it has been mean of me to allow you to feel it was your fault we left London."

"Oh, do drop it, Beattie. You were right to think of coming here, and I was more than happy to . . . remember?

Imagine us living on into our dotage in one room in the Cromwell Road, those flights of stairs – that shared bathroom. Never mind the things we avoided . . . the Spanish flu after the first war and then the bloody Blitz in the second? We came here at the right time. You mustn't take on blame to yourself – and besides it worked for a long, long time. Your garden has fed us, and we have had a home here . . ."

"Thirty-four years of, more or less, happy times . . ."

". . .More or less? Thanks a bunch!" Dora nudged her and smiled. "'You are all heart,' as they say."

"But were we happy?" Unusually, Beatrix needed to seek out some reassurance, affirmation that her long-held perceptions were true.

"We found each other and that has been the happiest of all things. Where we have been, how our lives have been lived, are secondary to that one delightful happenstance," said Dora, stroking Beatrix's hand.

"Besides, your nerves couldn't have taken the Blitz," Beatrix teased, lightening the mood. Neither of them was especially fond of spending long in such an emotionally exposing conversation, but Beatrix was always the one to pack it in first.

"Well, I didn't do that badly during the never-to-be-forgotten evening at the Gateways. Remember us heading in that day? I mean what were we thinking of?

"The luck of the innocent."

"Or the insane?" laughed Dora sitting back down on her stool. "I remember getting to the club at opening time, I know that's right as we were keen not to be out late. It was all as usual, but then very early doors there came word from the street and if you went out you could hear the drone of the planes overhead and the bloody bombs beginning to fall. Do you remember the entire chorus line from

Applesauce arriving after the early show at the Empire 'cause one of them was a Gateways Les Girlie and dragged them all over to the club? And they struck up the piano and sang their brave little hearts out and the younger ones ended up doing knees-ups whilst we oldies drank toast after toast to anyone and anything we could think of. Gina let all the rules go out of the window and no-one got chucked out at midnight. Then Mary came in very flushed, having done a recce, and said it was all quiet ... horribly quiet ... and we could leave but no one wanted to leave so we all bedded down on the floor and we found rugs and blankets from Lord knows where and Smithy came over all soft and served tea through the night. Was Oliver there?"

"I don't recall," said Beatrix, trying hard to remember, as so much of that night was still as vivid to her as it was to Dora.

"I remember the dawn and us all departing quietly, going our separate ways and the streets silent and the atmosphere grim. We were lucky to be in Chelsea, weren't we, though it was a different story two days later – but do you remember getting to Marylebone and hearing about the devastation in the East End? People wandering about in shock – that silence you get. We made friends with strangers whilst other people lost their homes, their lives."

"*Applesauce*, now that was a truly terrible production," said Beatrix, prodding at an old bruise.

"Well, you never liked those type of review shows, did you? *More dramatic action ... less eyes and teeth,* you used to say. The number of things I went to on my own."

"You had an absolute ball because I left the *eyes and teeth* camp following up to you. Give me a good dose of Chekov any day."

"Typical of you. All that moaning on about sodding

Moscow. Vera said she loved the Blitz, loved the war. Best time of her and Mary's bloody lives she said."

Beatrix laughed. "Vera would!"

"Damn this drip," Dora said, taking her hanky out of her cardigan sleeve to wipe her nose and releasing a whiff of Eau de Cologne.

Dora took Beatrix's cold hand in her warm one and, though holding on to Beatrix more than leading her, she rose from the stool and waltzed her big bottom out from behind the counter to glide out onto an imaginary dance floor in the middle of the shop. They swayed gently in unison, feet slowly treading the boards.

"So that night might have scared the pants off us, but we'd had our moments before, back in the Smoke, hadn't we Beattie? Remember early closing days – shutting the shop on a Thursday afternoon and heading in for a three o'clock matinee, or going up to town for a Saturday night? La da da daa– Laa da da daa da da ... *Begin the Beguine* ... remember it Beattie? Remember dancing to that record at the Gateways? Seeing Artie Shaw and his orchestra performing it at the Hammersmith Palais? Gin and Bridge gatherings at Vera and Mary's? La da da da da ... how long now since we danced?"

"You were the one doing all the dancing! As I recall it I was just there to buy the drinks," Beatrix teased. "It must be at least eleven years since that last trip to the club ... toasting as the bombs fell ..."

"I really have deteriorated, haven't I?" said Dora, stopping the slow waltz to look down at her swollen feet. "I guess our last trip up to town was Mary's funeral ..."

"No, Vera's. Mary went first remember? Mind you it should have been Vera first, all those bloody fags she smoked."

"I tried to keep up with her, but you wouldn't let me!"

"Damn right – they stank to high heaven. How we survived in that windowless basement club is anybody's guess."

"Balkan Sobranie cocktail cigarettes – how stylish they were." Dora mimed an expansive puff. "Do you think we are the last of Les Girls?"

"Well, the club's still going."

"Jolly cheeky of Ted to give us that French nickname, but it fitted Gina's desire for everything to be demure and beneath the surface." and Dora's high heels began to step the beguine, her hips swaying to a far slower rhumba time than in her memory."

They separated, holding hands at arm's length and Dora turned in a small circle, bent slightly at the waist, but not without grace, before heading back to the security of Beatrix's arms. They simplified, slow-stepping to the beat in their own heads; Beatrix shut her eyes, as Dora rested her head on her shoulder. Dora was the dancer, the one on the dance floor hour after hour – the waltz and the samba, the lindy hop and the beguine. Beatrix had tried her darndest with both the dancing and the prep, the dressing up, the prinked hair, the lipstick, and the decisions to be made, but hour, after God damned hour of it all, left her cold in the end. Her tweed skirt and jacket made her feel comfortable, protected and truly herself, and her look had never changed. Though it was not as far as some of the butches took it, with their men's suits and ties, it was enough to identify her and ensure she was accepted. So she took to staying behind to look after the shop till closing on the Saturday, whilst Dora would go on ahead to Vera and Mary's to join in their prinking and preening, only meeting up at the Gateways. She'd had to admit they looked absolutely swell – and all the more so for being agreeably flushed with excitement. In the end, she took to leaning on the bar and admiring Dora and her gaggle of femmes in their fancy frocks from a distance, which she found far more pleasurable than joining in; she was, she discovered, happiest observing from the edge of an admiring crowd. On the edge of that crowd, she found the shyest of secret queers, Oliver.

"What a place that was – hearts filling with anticipation as we descended those perilous stairs, knowing we could be ourselves, no judgement, no questions asked," Beatrix said, stroking Dora's back.

Dora pulled her head up to look up at her and the slow dance stopped. "What are we going to do Beattie? I am sorry to have baulked at the last hurdle. I know I agreed not to change my mind again, but I just don't have the stomach. I'm not like you, I'm not brave."

"Come on, it's all right, I'm honestly relieved ... how could I not be in so many ways?" said Beatrix, trying to sound far more relieved than she felt. "I had a good think outside with the hens, just as you knew I would – life going on as always had its calming effect. We will come up with something."

The two women separated and returned to behind their counters. The return to the usual a relief, after such a display of indiscretion.

"You know, the horse came to me this morning? He came to me unasked," said Beatrix, after a long silence.

"Perhaps it was a sign he wants us to stay?"

"Perhaps, but we can't. I will phone Alice, in a while, I promise. She will be home getting Harold's lunch ready, no doubt. I'll try before my walk with Oliver. I am sure we can stay there together for a short time. Just because we don't know the answer yet, doesn't mean a plan won't emerge, does it?"

"What if you don't phone . . ."

"Dora what are you saying?" Beatrix dragged the stool from behind her counter to sit down beside Dora. "I don't want any more changes of heart – please Dora – I can't take it."

"No. But I won't face the bailiffs, or the crass stupidity of Miss Moyle. Let's just leave here tonight – or very early tomorrow morning – last bus, or first. Just go. Run away. Leave the shambles and the debts – disappear. I can't bear to watch as they take it all over. What's the point? And anyway, I don't believe Alice will leave us out on the street if we just turn up. Might even be better – just turn up out of the blue."

"Let me speak to Alice, it's better if I do. See what she says, then let's plan the next piece of the jigsaw. Meanwhile – and please don't upset yourself, I will sort it, I promise – but we have another issue. I posted a letter to Oliver this morning. When I thought we were on Plan A."

"What letter to Oliver? What on earth did you do?"

Beatrix could feel this news pushing Dora into the very place she had just worked so hard to keep her from – the place where her nerves let rip and internal chaos reigned. "Please don't worry. I will sort it I promise. I will see him for our walk later as normal and I will explain that he is to rip it up when it arrives and not read it – that it was sent in error. He is an honourable man; I am sure he will do as I ask."

"What did you tell him in the letter . . . what did you say?"

"I told him what we had agreed – what we had planned to do today. I asked him to come and find us, make sure we were treated properly, with respect and with care – call Alice and tell her – the usual sort of things. I told him what to do about the funeral . . . the hens . . ."

"The HENS!"

"What to do with our wills . . . that sort of thing. Don't look at me like that, Dora."

"You had no right to do that without talking to me about it."

"But we did agree we would leave a letter for him . . . before you . . ."

"Yes, we agreed WE would do that – and I thought that WE would write that together. You took it into your own hands to write MY BLOODY suicide note! Good God, Beattie. What . . . possessed you to do THAT?" Dora got slowly to her feet by leaning on her counter.

Beatrix stayed sitting, blocking her way, speaking quietly. "Because . . . I suppose . . . because . . . I knew you never would."

"And so, you just did it anyway?"

The doorbell jangled. Beatrix picked up her stool and moved quickly back to her counter.

"Good morning, ladies. I have brought you some more hand-knits to sell for the poor Barnardo's boys. I must say you are my very top-selling shop!" Mrs Hodge bustled in, eyes down and busy about her own business. She rested her basket on the sweet shop counter and took off her head-scarf, which she shook out vigorously, before retying it under her chin. "What a morning for the weather, a misty dawn, a glorious sunrise and now a hail shower, whatever next?"

"Hail? Dear me. We didn't even notice it did we, Miss Veal? We've been so busy here what with one thing and another." It was fascinating watching Dora shift totally from furious wronged victim to shopkeeper though a four-sentence transition.

"No," Beatrix said quietly, remaining seated on her stool. Beatrix watched as Dora moved out from behind her counter and pushed her hands into the softness of the bundle of multi-coloured mittens, hats, and bootees in Mrs Hodge's basket, each tied together by their woolly drawstrings – the regular replenishment of the display a deep insult to her now redundant post office counter. Of all the people to break into this moment it was William's mother, bearing more disgusting little itsy, bitsy, bobitty, knits.

"Well, Mrs Hodge, it must be hard work for you, but your knits just fly off your counter don't they, Miss Veal? Such a lovely collection of colours as well, the pinks and blues are very fetching, don't you think?" said Dora, her eyes twinkling, evidently enjoying every moment of annoying Beatrix by holding up a particularly disgusting blue bobble hat, forcing her to acknowledge and admire. Her revenge would be protracted and various; it always was.

"I feel it is the least I can do for the poor orphaned boys."

"Yes, all those poor dear boys . . ."

"And girls," said Beatrix, to prove she was still up for the fight.

"Well, of course, and the girls," said Mrs Hodge, who was a woman who enjoyed a pointed remark herself. "There must be a considerable collection in this boy's charity box for the orphans by now, as we have sold so many. You'll need to get Barnardo's to come and empty it, Miss Veal," she said, without any sign of embarrassment at bragging about the popularity of her own knitting.

Beatrix looked anxiously over at the statue of the Barnardo's boy in the corner, his painted brown hair flat to his head, his cherry lips pleading, his calipered leg for all to see, presenting his collection box between tightly clutched hands. Please God, despite all that do-good zeal, William's mother did not have the strength to go over and lift it.

"We simply can't match the demand with the supply," Beatrix said, following on with a tight smile at Dora, "Perhaps you would like to tell Mrs Hodge who our many customers are, Miss Ham?"

"Oh, many and varied, many and varied I dare say," said Dora, retreating to behind her counter to adjust her sweet jars, as if they needed any. Mrs Hodge began to lay out her newly made garments from the tangled pile on Beatrix's counter. Four bright-yellow bobble hats as well as the blue, a long purple scarf, and many pairs of little lacy bootees and mittens – the pointless type that can't possibly stay on a baby's hand or foot for more than a minute before disappearing into a hedge. A fact known to a childless Beatrix, ignored by Mrs Hodge. The poor must always be grateful however pointless the gift.

"Well, it's quite a system we now have isn't it, ladies? The vicar's wife told me the other day she has more wool for me, as she has had so many donations of unrepairable garments. She'll wash it and re wind it into balls and let me know when she is done. I don't take the dark stuff – she gives that to the Women's Guild in Great Missenden. I just take the bright. I love a brighter knit."

"Now dear, what else can I get you?" asked Dora, who was looking even more flushed in the cheek – if that were possible. She plainly wanted Mrs Hodge gone – so she could continue the row about the letter. "Would you like to try the sherbet lemons for a change?"

"No, just a quarter of dollies, if I may," said Mrs Hodge, handing over her ration book to be stamped. "Anyone would think the ruddy Germans won the war the way this Labour government's going about it; this rationing can't go on much longer surely. Can't help your business much, now, can it? I mean our butcher's shop does all right on the rations, though nothing like the old days, but everyone needs a bit of meat don't they. Whereas with sweets ..."

"It's a disaster," said Beatrix, without looking up from pushing the lumps of wool to the corner of her counter, as far away from her as possible.

"Well, you must be hoping for Churchill then, Miss Veal. He will put a stop to that nonsense and quite a few other things as well, make no mistake."

"Well actually ..."

"I don't doubt," said Dora, giving Beatrix the look, which it was wiser not to ignore under the circumstances, whilst quickly tipping the quarter of pink-and-white sweets into a small paper cone and twisting the top. She leaned forward as if there were other customers that might over-hear her. "I must apologise, we rather gave William the run around this morning – after asking him to come early we both overslept – can you imagine! I do hope he wasn't too put out?"

"I really have no idea, that boy lives in a dream world of his own." Mrs Hodge pushed her ha'penny onto the counter, with her ration card for Dora to stamp. "Must rush, let me know if you need any more garments sooner than normal, otherwise I'll be back in a month with some more." And with that she was gone.

The bell jangled to a stop. The silence that followed was full of deadly anticipation. Dora stood, pressing her hands into fists on her counter.

"Do you have to try and pick a fight with everyone who comes in here today? Everyone I have tried to make a life with over the years?"

Here we go. The big speech followed by the flounce out. Beatrix 'girded her loins' as D.H. Lawrence might well have said in *Sons and Lovers*, the book she must remember to return to Oliver today.

"This . . ." continued Dora, casting her hands round the shop, "this . . . in case you have not noticed . . . is . . . my . . . life. Whilst you are outside picking greenfly off your tomatoes and wandering the hills and fields with Oliver, I have made this my life."

"Oh Dora, please do spare me the dramatics. Come off your high horse for goodness' sake. Really? You enjoy your little interludes with Molly and her ghastly pal? I am sorry about the letter and I promise I will deal with it. It was wrong of me, and I am sorry. Honestly there was nothing in it you would have objected to – it was merely factual. I just wanted to make sure we were treated with respect, and you had already agreed that Oliver would be the perfect person to ensure that was the case."

"Kind, slightly damaged, malleable, queer man – you know how to pick them don't you?" Dora said, standing her ground, whilst holding on to her counter.

"That comment isn't worthy of you, really it isn't." Beatrix tried a distraction, a lightener, to get things back on track. "Come on duckie . . . time to reveal all . . . where exactly have all the disgusting little woollen bobities been going?"

"The vicar." Dora found the good grace to look guilty. "I would have you know he is perfectly happy with the arrangement, as am I, but it's probably best you don't enquire further."

"Oh no, please don't tell me he is shipping them to those orphanages in Africa he goes on and on about?" Beatrix had a vision of rows and rows of tiny, helpless orphaned babies, bundled up in woollen hats, scarves, mittens, and bootees in disgusting colours on every head, foot and hand. Perhaps they might get badly dehydrated and die of heatstroke? Poor mites. Bloody Mrs Hodge, bloody empire, bloody do-good vicar. "Why on earth send woollen knits to Africa?"

"Surely it gets cold at night. It does get cold at night in certain places, I am sure. Besides it doesn't matter really, does it? Does it?" Beatrix could hear in Dora's voice that her firm ground was shifting under her swollen feet.

"Well of course it matters if you are running a potentially – it now occurs to me – very likely criminal deception. Mrs Hodge thinks you are selling the knits for charity and putting the money in the Barnardo's boy – when all along you are passing them over to the vicar for free. You don't suppose the vicar's wife is in on the act and knows full well what is happening when she gives Mrs Hodge the wool, do you? My goodness, perhaps she is simply unwinding the knitting and giving Mrs Hodge back the same wool!"

"Oh, very droll! What does it matter if the money goes in the Barnardo's boy in the corner, or the knits go to the poor in Africa? What difference does it make?" asked Dora, looking startled by the notion that in fact none of these knits were going anywhere, through the added potential betrayal by the vicar's wife.

Beatrix laughed. "Dora, for goodness' sake! What a tangle. What a tangle of bright pink and blue wool you are in. I don't think you are about to be arrested by the Barnardo's police, really, I don't."

Dora picked up the coin lying on her counter and staggered to her till by the scullery door. She took out the little money that was in there and purposefully made her way over to the silent boy in the corner holding out his empty box.

"You need this far more than we do actually dear," she said as she put Molly's and Mrs Hodges' money and the night float into the boy's ever-hopeful tin – each coin dropping with a clunk. "There you go my duck," and she gave him a pat on the head, before using it as a push-off to launch herself.

"You almost got me there," she said, and exited the room crabwise with her head held high.

Beatrix ran her fingers over the familiar grain of the wood of her counter, tracing the ink spots and scratch marks with her finger; all those years of service measured by these old battle scars. The devastating letter from the GPO arrived two Christmas' ago with a lack of consideration for the season, nestling on the door mat, concealed between a couple of Season's Greetings cards. The message couldn't have been colder and starker . . .

To enable a post-war centralisation of the services that will be provided by the returning male workforce all non-establishment temporary contracts are to be terminated . . . your status of Sub-Post Office Postmistress to be made redundant . . . shop and house to be sold due to the consequential rationalisation of service.

She didn't tell anyone, she didn't complain – when they asked her, she said she had decided to give it up – too much trouble, better off without it in her life.

A tidy little man came to collect her official seals, till and certificates and declare her . . . if only they knew how anti-establishment she was . . . 'non-establishment services redundant'.

Along with other rural reductions your service will be offered by a larger facility in Great Missenden . . . as you are aware all temporary, non-establishment contracts carry no pension, no redundancy pay . . . keep your financial records . . . the books . . . minimum seven years . . . destroying them might be regarded as a criminal offence. And then the sting in the tail . . . *this rationalisation allows men to be released to fulfil heavy industry duties . . . not applicable in your case and age . . .our thanks . . .loyal years of service . . .*

He spoke as if reading from a script. She sat stiff-backed at her own table in her own scullery, signing away her income along with her purpose in life. She gave him nothing, so why had she so foolishly yearned for some sign of understanding? Some recognition of the disaster this spelled. What would it have cost the government to allow her to keep going? This wasn't about the rationalisation of a service and the post-war effort; this was about ripping the heart out of her life and the life of the village. She was declared officially superfluous, her previous contributions forgotten – her reduction a necessary part of the move forward to peacetime. She was the fool not to see it coming, but then again it had lasted so long and who was to say a third war was not just around the next corner and women needed again? She should never have agreed to take over the non-establishment terms of her predecessor Harry Henderson, lost in his own termination in the Great War, but used her power to her advantage when she'd had it.

The tidy little man gave her not one jot of empathy (what could you expect from a man with such small feet?), but asked her to *sign here and here and here, Miss Veal, and I can be on my way.* He shook her hand, and she closed the shop door quietly enough behind him – its etched glass *Post Office and Sweet Shop – Madams Veal and Ham* now nothing but a humiliating lie.

Beatrix looked at her watch – just after ten o'clock. The unwitting Oliver would be calling for her at one o'clock for their Thursday afternoon walk, a type of physical activity that Dora went a very long way to avoid, her dizzy spells having developed a particular love of an early closing afternoon. Perhaps she should have shared their troubles with Oliver before today? Shared what was happening to them? Told him about why the post office side of the business closed? Now she came to think about it, in all the years they had known each other they had never talked about anything deeply personal. Though the banter they had exchanged at the Gateways club, as they watched the others dance from the side-lines at the bar, had progressed after Oliver moved here. On their walks they had found political perspective – from the inevitable war news and its aftermath to a shared frustration in the failures of post-war governments. Through fiction they analysed other people's lives and motivations, debating the themes in the novels they swapped on their weekly walks; thus, through fantasy and reality, they negotiated a common ground. They shared a loathing for village gossip, though she suspected he used some of its characters in his occasional short stories. He said he sold them to make ends meet, but she had never seen his name against any of the stories she read in the magazines, borrowed from their shelves during long afternoons in the shop. He had always been careful not to offer to show her any of his work and as a result she wondered if he feared she would be too critical a judge. She hoped not.

At some moment on their walk today she would have to broach the tricky subject of the letter, face up to the truth with Oliver. She had been reassured in her fear of the shame in the discovery of their death – reassured to know it would have been him that would come to find them first and be in control of the postscript of their lives – so reassured in fact that until now she had not allowed herself the intrusion of wondering what it would be like for him. Now, in the unveiling of this prospect and facing up to the consequences of her previous plan, she feared his reaction;

though as he had unwittingly been made redundant in this role, she regretted having to raise it at all. Then there was the matter of what next – the void of any satisfactory solution exhausted her. Certainty of death had its advantages: unlike the living you were no longer responsible for tying up your own loose ends.

In this way, wondering, wondering what she might have done differently and how to fix everything, Beatrix passed a quiet time, listening to the voices of yesterday's customers as they passed by the shop.

Chapter Four

Beatrix sat down next to the small telephone table in the hall and dialled the three letters and four numbers that she knew only too well; though they spoke irregularly their means of communication was ingrained into her memory. She listened to the purr purr down the line, promising herself that if it rang more than ten times, she could replace the receiver and tell Dora she'd tried. How many times would Dora make her dial again till giving up? How many rings . . .

"Durham 9058?" Alice's voice sounded curt — no, anxious — as if this intrusion of a telephone call were automatically a threat.

"Hello, Alice. It's Beattie."

"Beattie. Good Lord. Beattie? What's up — something happened?"

"No, ah, no. Nothing shocking. How are you?"

"How are we? Well, we are as you might say, 'fine'. We are fine, Beattie."

That was it. There was nothing, nothing, that Beatrix could think of to ask about their little life — how was the walk to the shop on the corner? How was the breakfast they had just eaten? How was . . .

"Harold's chest?"

"Oh, you know he battles on like he always has. It's a terrible affliction and he is so good about it. When I think of ..."

Here we go, thought Beatrix. When Alice thinks of all the men ...

"When I think of all the men who have been made to suffer in this way and still the pit does nothing, admits nothing. Daddy knew and God knows he tried in his day to make them see how it was connected. They couldn't give a damn, and the longer it goes on they care even less of a damn than the year before. It's a losing battle as each man goes down before him."

There was silence. A coldness drifted down the line. Ask me how I am, thought Beatrix, it's the done thing. Where had the little girl, whose wriggly warm hand used to reach for hers at surprising moments, gone? She waited; surely it would come.

"How's things with you, Beattie?"

This was the moment to lay it on thick – but not so thick that Dora sounded like a case for a nursing home. She must step carefully here now ...

"Well, you know, Dora's nearly seventy-five now and I am beginning to think the shop is too much for her. She's brave, but she is also getting tired, well we both are ..." Beatrix laughed to the silence at the end of the line. "We're none of us in the first-flush of our youth now are we ...?"

"Speak for yourself old girl – you have six years on the clock ahead of me. I was saying this only the other day – we are all as young as we feel and I certainly ..."

"But certainly, time is slipping – ticking I mean – onwards for us here and for Dora, especially." Beatrix pushed on, determined not to be led off the point. "In fact, we, Dora and I, we have been wondering what we should do . . . do about the shop . . . It really can't go on like this any longer."

"You're surely not thinking of giving it up because of Dora? Why? Let her go her own way and you carry on. You talk in such a maudlin way Beattie, you always have. *Seize the day* as Daddy would have said. You will keep going, won't you? Surely you could manage on your own? Or get a young assistant in to help, if Dora can't cope anymore?"

"Well, under other circumstances that might have been possible."

"What do you mean?"

"In other circumstances than we find ourselves in . . . right now."

"Right now?"

"Right now, we have found ourselves . . . found ourselves . . ." how could she even begin to say it? ". . . Found ourselves . . . I mean it's ridiculous but there it is . . . out of favour . . . with the bank . . . and unable now to pay any rent . . . to such an extent that we are having to close the shop and with immediate effect."

"What are you talking about . . . with immediate . . .? You don't pay any rent – the shop and the house go with the job you always said. Oh, Beattie, what on earth has been going on?" There was a touch of kindness. Not a softness, Alice was never soft, but a concern in her voice – a chink of hope.

". . .We were tootling along OK, well just about OK, but then two years ago . . . just before Christmas . . . which was infuriating as it always was the time of year with the most activity to tide us over . . ." don't cry . . . hold it, hold it, Beatrix fought it, "I never told you . . . for shame . . . I was released from my duties as a sub-post mistress and then the

house and shop sold by the GPO to a ghastly local man ...
and the ongoing rationing ... even after the war ended ...
because people were so bloody stupid ... and that tipped the
balance out of kilter to such an extent that ... we ran out of
our savings ... and have got ourselves into quite a pickle."

"You never said ... why have you never said?"

"The rent, in itself, might not have been so much of a
problem, but the old bank manager – who was a friend
and a good man – was replaced by his son a couple of years
back – a total bastard, not to put too fine a point on it,
and ... well ... the bank won't advance any more money
and wants the overdraft repaid and have decided to call in
the bailiffs and the landlord has called time on the tenancy."

"How long have you known things were this bad?"

"Oh ... well ... as I said, bad for a while but then really
bad ... about a year."

"About a year?"

"Well yes. I mean of course we hoped things would
take a turn, we hoped we could persuade Terry, Terry
the landlord, to waive the rent for a bit because with a bit
of an uptick things would improve, and they have been a
bit better recently, they truly have, but Terry doesn't care.
Terry is on a mission to shut us down, do it up as a house
again and sell it for a mint."

"My God, Beattie, what will you do – I mean – what do
you have to go forward?"

"It wasn't exactly much – but it's all gone now." Here it
was, here came the moment of truth. "We have nothing.
The business is bankrupt, and we are the business. We have
nothing and we must leave."

"How soon?"

"Tomorrow."

"Tomorrow? What are you saying? Tomorrow? How on

earth have you let it get this bad, Beattie? Where will you go and what will you do?"

"Well, that's why I am calling you."

The silence was absolute. Beatrix counted the beats one, two, three, four, five . . .

"You surely don't expect to come here, do you?"

Beatrix wound her finger through the black coils of the telephone receiver wire. Back and forth she looped the loop. She could hear Dora cooing away to someone in the shop through the closed scullery door. She was spinning upwards, up from the telephone table in the hall, up through the roof. She could see the hens way down below her, pecking on the dry dust, for no grain. She could see the horse look up from the field and stare at the house, but no one came. She was floating way up high, safe, out of it all, a tiny atom in the sky. "Well, we were hoping . . . just for a time . . ."

"We? No Beattie. You surely don't mean Dora too?"

"Alice, what am I to do? We came here together, we set up the business together, we have a partnership. I can't just drop her now things have turned out as they have. It's not Dora's fault. None of this is Dora's fault."

"I'm not for one moment suggesting that it is, but she is not your responsibility now Beattie. You must look after number one here. Has she no means of her own? No family?"

Beatrix wound the cord tight. That's right you haven't a clue have you, dear Alice, not a clue. Never cared, never showed the least bit of interest in my life. Never pulled your head up from the drudgery of fixing and feeding that no-good husband of yours, who wheezes his way down the road to the pub and the bookies, a little fix on the tote what harm can it do. Yet more money down the relentless drain that is Harold. You married beneath you Alice and for what? Never once thought to ask – where is the love in your life Beattie? Never once. Dora might not be wealthy but at least she had class.

"Alice, she has nothing."

"I . . . am I to understand from this, that you are asking if you could come here? That both of you could come here?"

"You are." Nothing for it, what is said cannot be unsaid.

"Beattie, how on earth do you think that could work? We only have the one spare bedroom . . . ."

"We will happily share. We both have our weekly pensions to contribute to the household and . . ." Beatrix knew this next would not be believed, but she had to believe it for herself if nothing else . . . "It's only for a short time till we work out what to do next . . . work out where we go next."

"Well, both of you to a grim public nursing home, I don't doubt," said Alice, bitterly. "And then I will have that on my conscience. It's not kind of you Beattie, not kind at all, to put me in this position – to put Harold and me in this position. I am not at all sure, really . . . I don't know what he will say when I suggest this. I mean what about all your stuff?"

"We will leave all but two suitcases here."

"Everything? Is it really tomorrow – why tomorrow?"

"The bailiffs are coming."

"You and your proud ways. Why have you not spoken about this before? Two years and nothing said. You are too proud, Beattie, and that always has, always will be your undoing. Too proud for a man, too proud for a proper job, too proud to live in Durham . . . the big smoke was calling you . . ."

"As in pride comes before a fall . . .?"

"As in just that."

"Well thanks – little sister."

"Don't mention it."

Was that a glimmer of humour, of understanding, of blood-ties and family? Don't push it, Beatrix thought. Let the line hang.

"Well, this is quite something to take in. I really don't know what to say."

"Please Alice. Just don't say no. Not now – even if you mean to say it. Talk to Harold and call me back later this afternoon. Don't tell me now what you think, please. I must go back in the shop and tell Dora something. Give me that. That we have spoken, that you are thinking about it, that you will talk to Harold. Even if you don't, even if you keep this to yourself and just call me later and say no. I just need, right now I need, to have something to cling on to – for Dora. Can you at least agree to that?"

"Why does she mean so much to you? Silly old lah-di-dah that she is. She should have died by now and left you her money, after all you'd have done it for her if she had looked after you all this time."

"You can blame her all you like – though living long is hardly a sin, really, is it?"

"I mean, I always thought she was the one with the money – has it truly all gone? Or is she hiding some from you?"

"Alice there never was much – it's truly all gone. Everything is all gone trying to save the shop."

Beatrix untangled the mangled cord and replaced the receiver on the black Bakelite telephone. She straightened the notepad and pen and ran her finger round the fringe of the little table light. Specks of dust, minute particles of the past, fell onto the polished tabletop. Where had she read it? That your house dust was made from flecks of your own dead skin – slowly filling up your home with your own discarded past self? Discarded elements of Dora and Beatrix, left behind to fall between the cracks in the floor-boards, waiting for new owners to begin shedding a new layer of their own skin, pile upon pile of human remains. The shop had fallen silent; Dora would be reading the local rag. Beatrix must put on her hopeful face – the one she had worn thin with overuse, smoothing away the terrors. In her heart of hearts, she knew what Alice would say – if, and when, she rang.

"Hey there," said Dora, not looking up from her mag. "How's trix?"

The sun was making a good show of penetrating the frosted windowpane in the door, the day building to one perfect for a refreshing walk.

"Well, 'Trix' has done her duty and telephoned Durham."

Dora looked up, worried. "And how did Durham take it?" Having insisted on this course of action, it was clear she now feared the consequences. Always the same with Dora – winning the argument was one thing – being responsible for the outcome was another. "Who answered the telephone?"

"Alice. You surely don't think Harold – far too much like hard work."

"What did you tell her, how much did you say?"

"There seemed little point in dressing it up." Beatrix moved behind her side of the post office counter. "I told her the truth. That we are bankrupted and to be evicted."

"Was she angry you hadn't told her before?"

"No."

"Hurt?"

"Not exactly."

"What then?" This was how it always was. Dora pushing, pushing; Beatrix had to come up with something.

"I don't' know – perhaps a bit shocked?"

"I bet she was shocked. What did she say?"

Beatrix sat down on her stool and turned the date on her date stamp, saying nothing, as she had nothing to say.

"Beattie, for goodness' sake don't make me drag it out of you line by line. This is how it always is. Be kinder. I would give you a blow-by-blow account of the call, whereas you make me ask for every single detail. Tell me what she said when you asked if we could come tomorrow ..."

"I can't remember."

"Remember, or recount? Of course, you can remember – please recount."

"Please leave it, Dora. She said she would talk to Harold and call back later today."

"That was it?"

"That was it."

"Did she indicate anything – in her words – her tone?"

"Nothing. Don't harangue me. She gave no indication."

"OK, well then try this. What do you think she will say – when she calls back?"

"Dora, for goodness' sake – I did as you asked, I called her. I asked."

"Did you say both of us are to come and tomorrow?"

"Of course, I did. Let it rest please. You are doing your best to give me one of your headaches."

Dora looked as if she wanted to push the point but resisted the temptation.

The shop bell jangled. Beatrix looked up to see a crippled elderly man in a grey suit and black trilby hat entering the shop. *Daddy ... Daddy there is a sick man at the door come to see you; Never ever say that in his hearing Beatrix – you must say there is a gentleman come to see you!* The gentleman walked with a twisted gait greatly assisted by two sticks, as if his hips and his legs had been welded together as one solid piece, requiring him to use all the force his arms could muster to propel himself into the shop. Following two steps behind was a younger gentleman, a good-looking man of about thirty in a brown lounge suit and a similar trilby.

"Good day, ladies," said the elder, revealing a strong cockney accent. Having come to a stop in the centre of the shop he held himself up by means of a stick pressed into each armpit and with a clever bending manoeuvre he took off his hat; his hair was slicked-back in the old-style, his grey moustache a pencil line drawn across his top lip.

"Good day gentlemen, how can we help?" Beatrix got in first; Dora smiled her most welcoming smile, there was something beguiling about them both.

"Well, we haven't come in to buy anything specific. We was in the area, and I persuaded my son here to stop the car and call in, on the off chance, very much on the off chance, that I might find the wife of an old pal of mine still here, or perhaps still living in the local area? A Mrs Henderson? Mrs Harry Henderson?"

Beatrix looked at Dora; it had been at least thirty years since they had heard that name.

"Oh, but she no longer runs the shop – it is ours. We came here in 1917 – after, after the family left."

"The post office, or the area?"

"Both."

"Oh, I see. I thought as much when I saw the sign on the door." He turned to the younger gentleman. "You were right son." He looked back at Beatrix – his china-blue eyes piercing. He must have been quite a looker in his day. "By any chance do you know where she is?"

"I am sorry to say that we don't." Beatrix wasn't sure they should just pass on Sarah Henderson's parent's address without good reason and besides they must be long gone – and her found a new life entirely. The gentleman looked at his son again, then regarded his hat.

"Can we ask why you are looking?" said Dora.

Beatrix knew she would also want to be helpful, he looked so sad.

"I met Harry in '13. We had some times together in the Royal Engineers, I can tell you. I was telling my son here all the stories and it got me wondering what had happed to his wife. I knew he ran the post office here with her before the Great War. Like I said, we was touring the area – visiting some relatives in Amersham and I persuaded Joe here to make a diversion and just come in on the off-chance."

Beatrix came out from behind her counter and offered the gentleman her stool.

"Please do take a seat Mr . . .?"

"Wilkins. Don't mind if I do – though it doesn't seem right to take one from a lady."

"Think nothing of it," said Beatrix, wondering how to broach the news she feared she must give. "The thing is Mr Wilkins . . . I am very sorry to say that we took over this place after it had closed down. Harry's wife and small daughter left after . . . after . . . she tried to run it on her own for a while . . . after Harry . . . didn't make it back."

"Well, that is kind of you to feel you must tell me gently – but I know all about Harry. I was there when he copped it, and though we never found him, I was able to make sure his name is on the memorial out there at Thiepval and on the Post Office Circular's role of honour as well. I wrote to her when I was de-mobbed, and though she replied nice enough, she said she didn't need to meet me. Don't blame her, but despite that I couldn't resist trying to make contact one last time," he said, clearly working the news round in his head that she was unreachable. He looked at his son again, shrugged and then glanced down at his own polished brogues. His sticks splayed out from under his arms, like a pair of extra legs. "I am glad that you are here – reopened it. Lovely spot. So, you have run this place since she left?"

"Since we came in '17 – though sadly the post office element is now closed," said Beatrix.

"I was a post office worker myself," he said, brightening at the familiarity of comrades. "Sorting office in Mount Pleasant, in London. This one closed now you say?"

Here we go, thought Beatrix. "Yes, it closed down the Christmas before last . . ."

". . . So, you met Harry in France and his name's on the memorial at Thiepval?" Dora interrupted. "I should say my parents were French and though I was brought up in London my grandmother lived close by to Albert, so I know a little more than the average about that part of France." Though she was adding a degree of complexity in bringing her own history into the mix, Beatrix was grateful Dora was at least pulling the story forward and getting him off the post office line of enquiry.

"We met before that actually," he continued, back in charge. "I'd got myself signed up for the Post Office Rifles summer camp in '13 – thought it a bit of a laugh because it was two weeks off in Eastbourne. Lovely bit of the country, not sure if you know it? We PORs did a bit of training, had a lark about, there were socials and sporting events. Harry had done the same from here – he told me it was a good crack as the missus was impressed, whilst he looked on it as a two-week break from her and the kid. I don't mean to imply he wasn't a good family man – he loved that girl all right – but you know ladies how it is … all nappies and washing and all that."

"We can only imagine," said Dora, with a smile at Beatrix.

"Anyways," said Mr Wilkins, sailing on regardless, "a year later when the war came along, we was recruited into the Royal Engineers Special Reserve Postal Section – the first line of defence for the post office – or the last – depending on how you looked at it. We was actually on our way to the old Eastbourne summer camp in August '14 when the war broke out. Harry and some of 'em was sent home awaiting orders, some of us like myself was back to Mount Pleasant, intercepting suspicious letters, getting them off to the secret service no less – though frankly we didn't find that much. When that turned out to be a bit of a joke job, they packed us up and we were off to Kent and then to the advanced base post office at Le Mans.

Beatrix was beginning to wonder if offering the stool had been such a good plan after all. Mr Wilkins was in for the long haul and so were they. She prayed Dora did not start offering tea. Joe was moving gently from foot to foot; she hoped he would find a way to extract his father without embarrassment.

"It seems funny now don't it, to be talking about a more than decent postal service from home and back all through the Great War, but that is what we delivered didn't we ladies? Those boys depended on their mail as much as their rifles – brought every day with their evening meal regular as clockwork. Harry was posted from here – and joined me – by that time we was set up nicely in Boulogne."

"It was as efficient a service as was running in the UK," said Beatrix. There was no point in checking the man, he would tell his story in his own way.

"Oh, my word yes. Letters posted here were reaching the men at the front in two days and visa versa. Incredible when you think of it now really wasn't it? And parcels too – five million of them we managed one bloody Christmas! Sorry for the swearing ladies. You'd have thought the Americans would have learned something from us and made a better job of it when the second war came along – what a mess. I learned from a mate up north recently there were seventeen million undelivered parcels and letters in Birmingham waiting for delivery to and from US servicemen on the front line. So they had a load of Negro American servicewomen come over here and sort it all out for them. Terrible mess – with biscuits and cakes and the like all rotting and the warehouse full of rats. Did a damn good job at redirecting it all those women did. My mate said, very impressive indeed. I mean you women, you made up the war effort in equal measure and thanks to you we did it not once, but twice."

"Don't mention it," said Beatrix.

"Of course, the bad bit of the job for us back then in France was maintaining the cards on the whereabouts of the wounded and the notifications to be sent back home of the dead and the missing, that was the worst – reading and then returning the letters home that were never going to be read, or visa versa and delivering home letters from soldiers that were already dead. We could see the numbers – we could see how bad it was. Dreadful. We were safe where we were, but that really got to me and Harry. We felt bad that we was having such a cushy time of it, really we were. So, when the big push started to be talked of in '16 we signed up for some frontline work helping with communications. Crazy now to think of it – but we felt so bad."

"So, you both got taken down to the front line to the Somme area?" Beatrix tried to jump him forward once

again to the inevitable end before the tricky moment –
given Sarah's reaction to his letter they would not give him
her last known address.

"Yes, we was stationed as you say 'mam," Mr Wilkins
gestured to Dora with his hat, "As you say, in that neck of
the woods that you know, outside Albert and then walked
up to the front line. That July morning, we were checking
the communications lines, running fresh ones through
the trenches, when it happened. I wasn't with him. I was
further along in another trench when I heard it land and I
thought it must've took out quite a few. It kicked off big
time I can tell you after that – I was wondering what the
bloody hell to do for the best when this explosion knocked
me clean off my feet and did me legs for good. They sent
me up to the dressing station and that was when I found
out about Harry. Got him in one. I dare say it blew him
to bits, poor sod."

There was a silence. Beatrix wondered what to say, 'we
are sorry for your loss' didn't feel right at all.

Dora did her best. "It was a terrible time wasn't it – and
then for it to happen again in our lifetime seems incredible,
doesn't it?"

"Terrible," said Mr Wilkins. "What happened to your
family? Your grandmother was from that area you said?"

"She had a farm outside Albert and fled when it became
requisitioned as part of the garrison arrangements. She spent
her final days living with relatives of her late husband in
the south. I knew the house, only as a child mind, but I
believe the farm was damaged beyond repair at some point.
To my shame I haven't been there, though I think I have an
uncle on the memorial at Albert. Goodness me, I have not
thought of her, my *grand-mère* and that farm, for such a long
time. How wonderful that you should come by."

87

"Dad, I think we have disturbed these nice ladies long enough, don't you?"

"Yes, yes, of course," said Mr Wilkins, not moving from his stool and looking round the shop. "We should, of course we should buy some sweets. Joe what would you like? How's about some barley sugar sticks, you used to love 'em."

"Don't mind if I do," said Joe, moving towards Dora, who was up and getting down the jar.

"A quarter of an ounce?" she said.

"Make it a half," said Mr Wilkins, "Go mad, why don't we!" And he laughed a good belly-laugh, the blue eyes back on form again. "So, you have a nice place here. Came in '17 and stayed. One bad bit of news for one is a good bit of news for the other – makes the world go round."

"Yes, well you saw an advertisement didn't you Beatrix? We wanted out of London, it felt like we could do something for the war effort here."

"Permanent?" said Mr Wilkins, looking straight at Beatrix.

"No, temporary."

"And they kept it like that?"

"Yes."

"I mean, I suppose you could see why. A man coming back from the front in '18 – some man might have wanted the place, but then there was the second one and the same again – men to the trenches, women to the benches as they said. So, I guess that is why they kept you on."

"Yes," said Beatrix.

"But then after that and no man given the gaff – my God that's thirty something years – and they kept you temporary? Shocking, but then our lords and masters at the GPO are shockers aren't they? Temporary – so no pension after all those years of service?"

"No," said Beatrix.

"And you said shut down year before last?"

"Yes," said Beatrix.

"Just like that. Well, I never." Mr Wilkins shook his head. "Bastards – sorry for swearing ladies."

"Bastards," said Dora and Beatrix in unison.

"Here's me card – somewhere in one of me pockets Joe for the stamp and what will that be?" Joe rummaged around and pulled out the ration book.

"Mr Wilkins, we could not possibly charge you a penny. It has been a delight to meet you and find out about Harry. We often wondered," said Dora, sitting back down on her stool.

"We never met Sarah, she was already gone when we came," Beatrix felt it only right to be honest about the address. She would hate for him to leave wondering and she trusted him to understand. "In fact, we do have a very old forwarding address for Sarah – her parents in Fleet, but after all this time they would no longer be alive, so I am sure it would not be any use to you and also . . ."

". . . No, no, you're all right there," said Mr Wilkins, pushing himself up from her stool. "No, this has been just what I needed – to find out what happened to the shop. He loved this place. I'm so glad you are here. Sarah needs to be left alone – she's an old woman herself, if she is even still with us, and she don't need silly old men like me dragging her back where she didn't want to be."

"Come on then Dad," said Joe, "Let's be off then."

"Very nice to meet you and good day ladies. A real pleasure and thanks for the sweets, most kind." Mr Wilkins replaced his hat and strutted slowly off the premises in his peculiar dancing manner. The doorbell rested back on its spring.

"What a wonderful thing to have happened today of all days," said Dora. "What a man. How has he managed to get about like that all these years? Those old boys were certainly made of tougher stuff than some we can think of. Brings back that play we saw at the Apollo, *Journey's End.* Do you remember it? Myrtle got us tickets for the day after the opening night. We didn't speak until we got on the train at Marylebone to get back here. First time it truly came home to me – how it was for those men and how much it damaged them, emotionally I mean. I wonder, how did Oliver do in the Great War? I've never asked."

"He's only forty-nine he was too young," Beatrix said, picking up her stool and putting it back behind her counter.

"My goodness he doesn't look it – I always had him down for older. Well, it must have been just as affecting in the second, though somehow it doesn't come over that way."

"He is such a private man I only know his age because Vera asked him straight out one night at the Gateways."

"Vera would." Dora shivered, as if someone had walked over her grave. "Harry blown to pieces out there in all that mud and muck and mess. All I have is happy memories of visiting my *grand-mère* in her farmhouse with geese that terrified me and chased me round the yard and goats that nibbled my petticoats and pushed their little pointy faces into my hand for food, and her standing with her big wide arms to greet me at the front door. She called me *mon petite chou* – her little cabbage – like every good French *grand-mère* would, and I called her *Mémé*. She was far more straightforward than my complicated mother, bold and widowed, brave, and strong – even as a child I knew she was far, far stronger than I would ever grow up to be. She made the best *gâteau battu* I ever tasted in my life. I used to sit on her lap in the kitchen and dip my fat hands into the warm cakey bread with a sweet-and-sour gooey rhubarb sauce to dip it into that she made especially for me."

"Did you used to go on your own – it sounds jolly like it," said Beatrix. Dora had never really opened up about this time before, something about Mr Wilkins had set her off.

"It's funny, I have no recollection of my parents being there, nor Matilde. Where were they? They must have been there, as I could never have got there on my own. Perhaps they took the baby Matilde off on a trip and left me with her as maybe I was too much of a bother. I wouldn't have minded one jot if they had. There's a photo of me and *Mémé* somewhere around here that my father took at that time with that box camera of his, but I haven't a clue where it is. You know that is something we have never discussed," Dora fixed Beatrix with a firm eye, "working out what to take – finding those important things. Now we are not going down with the ship we must do that today. Let's find the photo album. Maybe my programme collection? What else?"

Beatrix didn't answer. She didn't want to think what she might save to take to Durham and another life she never wanted to live; still alive and having to abandon the place and their possessions; it was hard to bear.

Dora let the question hang. After a while she said, "What time is it?"

Beatrix looked at her watch. "Twelve-fifteen." Then feeling mean that she had not replied, she tried to make amends with, "you mustn't worry, we have plenty of time left to find the things we need to keep."

"I know we have." Dora sat still for a moment, staring at

91

the door. "I say, let's do something utterly outrageous and close early, after all no one has come apart from Mr Wilkins since you left the shop to call Alice."

"I thought I heard voices when I was on the phone?"

"Oh yes, sorry, 'no one' includes the vicar's wife."

Beatrix raised her eyebrows.

Dora lowered her pencilled ones into a frown. "Don't start that again now Beattie, please. She came in with that ruddy sausage dog of hers for a quarter of chocolate drops. Michael. I mean what kind of a name for a dog is Michael?"

"Why do we always say that?" said Beatrix, laughing.

"About Michael?"

"No, why do we call the vicar's wife 'the vicar's wife'?"

"Why do we call the vicar's wife 'the vicar's wife'? Because, stupid, she is the vicar's wife." Dora was looking at her quizzically.

"No. I mean she is Mrs Fonthill – but we never call her that. But then, we call Mrs Braithwaite 'Patience On Her Monument'. Just like with Mrs Eastry– because that's how she says History. What is her name by the way?"

"Patience? You just said it Beattie – Braithwaite!"

"No, Dora, Mrs Eastry?"

"I haven't a clue, nor do I care . . ." said Dora laughing.

"Then there was Mrs Spacious Room, your elderly French student."

"'Well now isn't this a lovely spacious room dear,'" said Dora with a terrible home counties squawk, "Her never-to-be-forgotten first comment on our bed-sit. My God, listening to her aural preparation each week was torture." Dora pulled her mouth into the shape of a letterbox, clutched her backside and squawked. "Eel eee yah ooone poisssion dance mone culottties."

"... Dora, you didn't teach her THAT?"

"No, but I wish now that I had."

"Nor, I hope, Winsome Winston, that put-upon boy who was picked up and dropped off by his brittle, no doubt fascist, father."

"No, I felt sorry for Winsome, I used to try and fatten him up with bread and sugar. Remember Woodbine Mary, who lived in the attic and always left us two single fags resting on a match outside our door? And then there was Mrs Pointy Shoes ..."

"Oh, stop it ... we never gave Terry a nickname ..."

"... Well we should. How's about Fat Greasy Bastard?"

"Not very inspired. What do you think they call us? Something terrible no doubt." Beatrix was enjoying this last dance. She looked at the brightly coloured knits that were still on her counter. "Why did she come?"

"Who?" Dora looked confused.

"The vicar's wife – do keep up dear – was she checking how well the reuse of her own wool had gone?"

"Sorry?" Dora looked confused, then laughed. "For goodness' sake drop it. No, like I said, just for the chockie drops. I gave her a bit over her ration. Anyway, Beattie, to get back to the point ... and the grand gesture. Let's shut up shop now, early on early closing day. Last time? Shut the shop for good. Whatever else we don't know today, that is the one thing we do know we are doing."

"After you, Madame Dora Ham, *la belle patronne de la confiserie*."

"And you, Madame Beatrix Veal, *la belle maitresse de poste* – who never learned to speak French!"

"Well, you never learned to cook."

"*Touche, ma chérie.*"

The two women walked to the shop door and Beatrix

flicked the snib to lock the latch for the last time. Dora turned the sign to say 'closed'. They pulled down the blind together.

"Can't help feeling that there should have been more to it than that," said Dora.

"Perhaps we should have sung something? Perhaps 'The Last Post?'"

"'Jerusalem'? 'Bring me my bow of burning gold, bring me my arrows of desire ...?'" Beatrix was surprised how bold her voice – how good – it sounded.

"'Goodbyee, goodbyee, wipe a tear, baby dear, from your eyeee'? One for Harry Henderson and Mr Wilkins?" Dora sang.

"You know, I thought shutting the door for the last time would break my heart – but all I feel is relief," said Beatrix. "No more pretending, no more anticipation. Done."

"Do you mind if I sit down, I'm coming over all queer – as the actress said to the bishop," said Dora. Her sweaty palm clung onto Beatrix's hand, as she led her back to her stool. "No, not here ... let's go into the scullery darling."

Beatrix led Dora through the darkened shop and sat her down at the table. She handed over her hanky, for Dora to wipe her dampened brow.

"Glass of water?"

"Thank you," said Dora, looking pale and sipping her water. "Don't fret, I'm fine. Just pulling your attention onto me as usual. You were right after all, silly to have that fudge on an empty stomach."

"Fancy an egg?"

"I do – but first I'm going to have a lie down upstairs with a book," said Dora, rising slowly out of her chair and gently touching the doorframe before she made her way into the hall. "What a luxury! But I don't feel guilty, not one bit. When you're back from your walk, we should dig out the mementos, pack our bags and decide what next."

"We'll do just that," said Beatrix, watching as Dora, hand-over-hand, made her way down the hall and began the climb up the stairs.

When at the top she called down, "Will you give Oliver my best, say we'll meet again – or some such?"

"I'll tell him you explicitly said so."

"Maybe you should walk up the hill at the back and into the copse, I don't think you've done that for ages."

"Funnily enough I was thinking the same thing myself."

"Do you think Alice will call back?" Dora asked.

"Let's see," said Beatrix. "Don't worry about it – as you say, what can she do if we just turn up? Sufficient unto the day and all that ..."

Dora's head disappeared then reappeared. "Beattie, before you go out would you check the meter on the gas? We were going to top it up remember, I might light up the fire. Make sure there's enough, would you? It's ruddy perishing up here."

"Will do – now get some rest."

"Funny that old boy turning up, wasn't it? Toodle-pip."

"Toodle-pip."

Chapter Five

Beatrix grabbed the copy of *Sons and Lovers* from the telephone table in the hall and put on her hen hat and coat.
Sometimes she was a little dressier for Oliver, sometimes
she wasn't. She glanced at the coin-operated gas meter in
the hall cupboard – still quite enough in there for Dora's
needs this afternoon, she could always top it up later. Don't
think too much about tomorrow – tomorrow will come
whatever the fretting.

She went out of their front door, past the closed shop and
down the lane that would lead eventually to Oliver's flat
above the butcher's. She passed by flintstone houses with
red-tiled roofs, set back behind well-cut hedges, which
boxed in the autumnal put-to-bed gardens, complete with
small garden ponds; it was a display of suburban perfection
that hid many faults. It had been a boon to her when Oliver
wrote and said he was moving to their village. A lucky
chance; she hoped he felt the same. Why did she do that?
She knew he felt the same. Though he was in his early-
thirties and she nearly fifty when they had met, they formed
an instant bond; Vera and Mary had introduced them in '35
at the Gateways, soon after it opened in between the wars.
How he knew them she had never asked. Of course, Oliver

didn't go there all the time – his regular stamping ground being the Kings Head in Cheyne Walk, down by the river. Beatrix and Dora missed those visits up to town. They had given it up after that incredible first night of the Blitz. Besides, the trek in from here had never been quite the same as living there, even if for a while they pretended it was.

Dora was right to say Oliver was more of a friend to Beatrix than to her. There was nothing specific in that – no animosity – though she recalled that Dora called her a camp follower at first, a mild jealousy getting the better of her. At the Gateways, Dora had her adoring crowd and Beatrix had Oliver; they all rubbed along well enough in each other's company, but if there was solace to be found in spending time alone with another, that was the natural split. As a couple they paired up with Vera and Mary. She knew it was tough for Dora after the move, as Vera and Mary and the crowd were in London, whereas Oliver had, by chance, moved into the village and their friendship even more firmly cemented as a result.

The flat was a little place that he and his older brother had inherited from an allegedly potty old aunt when she died in '46. His brother didn't want to live there – he had too cosy a life in Dawlish, so it suited him to let Oliver have it whilst they sorted out what next. That had turned out to be five years of wonderful company for her and she hoped for him. The flat was likely not much to speak of, though she had never been in it, but Oliver would have made it tidy and loved. He once let slip that he didn't have a cooker but did all his meals on a paraffin heater that also heated the sitting room. She wondered how he managed – she had never dared to ask – and she wondered what the butcher and his wife made of the quiet gentleman above them, who never went out without being properly attired. Oliver was always to be seen in a suit, tie and hat and in weather like today most likely a woollen coat, muffler and leather gloves. She felt bad about the hen hat – she should have made more of an effort; after all, this was to be their final walk.

When she turned the last corner, she was surprised to see he wasn't waiting for her outside the butcher's as usual. She checked her watch – just after one o'clock – so she headed up to the discreet door beside the shop window and gave it a hefty knock with the rapper. Above her head hung the shop sign – a butcher, she presumed Mr Hodge, chasing a terrified cockerel with a meat cleaver in both hands. She had told Oliver it gave her the willies and wondered how he could live with it dangling outside his window, which surprisingly made him laugh. The door opened almost immediately, as if Oliver had been waiting for her knock. Behind him she could see for the first time the steep stairs encased in a deep red linoleum that led to his eyrie, a small mirror, hatstand to the left and a doormat – onto which her letter would fall tomorrow morning – oh Lord, there was that as well.

"Hello there, Beatrix," he said. "I'm sorry I wasn't outside, but I had to nip back up to get your present," and he stuffed a small, oblong brown parcel into his coat pocket.

"A present? Why on earth would you be giving me a present?" said Beatrix, startled by the thought that she should have brought him one to mark the occasion of the last walk. "It's OK, don't look so worried, I haven't mistaken your birthday ... it's for later. I will explain. Is that my copy?"

"Oh yes, it is," said Beatrix, handing over *Sons and Lovers*. "Sorry I held on to it way too long ... but I did enjoy it."

Oliver looked doubtful. "Really? Hadn't thought it was your thing at all. You will have to tell me more as we go," and he put the book on the small ledge of the hatstand and shut the door. "What an afternoon! Perfect. Can't tell you how cooped up I have been feeling ... so glad you didn't cancel."

As he walked, he slipped on the anticipated muffler and hat, and pulled on his leather gloves; you are a dapper man, thought Beatrix, despite your shyness. Oliver still had a life before him and, though of course they had never discussed it, Beatrix had always hoped these walks would become redundant, by his moving on elsewhere; it wasn't right for someone of his age to be so alone. His soulmate must be out there somewhere, such a shame he had not yet turned up, but then he wouldn't be found hidden away above a butcher's shop in a suburban village. Now here she was, about to break it to him that she and Dora were the ones who were leaving. Letting Oliver down had stayed her tongue in sharing any troubles. She tried to recall why her previous state of mind, this silent behaviour, had been reasonable to her – the one in which she believed it was better for him to be kept in the dark – whereas at this moment of revelation it just felt patronising and selfish.

"Why would I cancel? I never cancel," said Beatrix, after slightly too long a pause.

"No, you never have. You, Beatrix Veal, are one of the most dependable women I know," he said.

"Well, better than Dora!"

"Oh way, way better than daffy Dora. But I feared, for good reasons of my own, that you just might cancel today because I needed you so much to come."

"Here I am," she said with a private smile, raising both her arms out wide and twirling round the once. This was Oliver, his gentleness made her free, made her gay, he relieved her of her burdens.

"Where to today? Your choice," he said, tipping his hat to her twirl.

"I chose last week. It's definitely your turn."

"Did you? – I don't recall." She knew he was lying, but it pleased her anyway.

"Your choice again then. My gift," he said.

"The mist was so compelling this morning out the back of our house. I fancy crossing the big field, then up to the copse, then into the woods beyond."

"Safe enough in the woods today – the bloody shooters will be at their desks in the city. Did you hear it at the weekend? One hardly believes there is a thing left alive up there – what with the firing of the guns and the baying of the dogs. Yet it seems they are so incompetent they don't catch a ruddy thing. At least that's what Mr Hodge tells me. Perhaps he is just making me feel better. I need to make further enquiries the next time he has some venison in, or a partridge strung up by the neck!"

"Perhaps."

They walked on in silence, safe in the knowledge that at some moment someone would break it when moved, over the stile and down the footpath that led to the big field. The sun had vapourised the mist to extinction and warmed the frost into dew, so that the grass on the path dampened their legs and the fronds of browning ferns bent with the weight of water droplets. Everything was shutting up shop, just the hips, haws and the nuts to show for the spring and summer that was.

Beatrix broke first. "Wonder if we shall see a buzzard up on the hill."

"I wonder," he said, "let's hope."

They turned through the gate into the field, shutting it

behind them. Now the going was tougher. The soil that had looked like soft demerara sugar from a safe distance earlier was now a blood-red clay, mixed in with flint stones, thrown up by the recent ploughing. It clung; weighing down their boots as they worked their way beside the hedge and tackled the incline, up the long sweep of the hill to the brow. At the top they turned their backs on the copse of trees to take in the view. The patchwork of wet and dry earth, topped by a dusting of chalk that marked the ploughed ridges left by the tractor lines, was magnificent in contrast to the watery blue sky; the sun had reached the climax of its height. Beatrix looked down at the row of houses that contained their little house with its shop and garden – all that hard work to tame that tiny patch. In the field below the horse walked forward, head down, grazing.

"Weren't we lucky that neither of those ruddy wars were fought here. We would be looking at all this in an entirely different way, wouldn't we? All that flesh and bone mixed into the mud."

"What on earth makes you think of that?"

"Oh, an old boy turned up at the shop this morning. Knew Harry Henderson who used to run the place before we came, was with him when he died at the Somme. Was lovely to meet him but it set me thinking – Dora's family were from that area, and she knew of its beauty."

"I didn't know that – about Dora's family being from round that way, nor that the man before you had been in the trenches, though of course it fits."

"Albert – poor benighted place found itself in the middle of it all. Her mother's side were never well-off after that – French country folk who lost everything. I can't help feeling we British were the lucky ones in terms of the Great War. We got off fairly scot-free – in terms of home turf, I mean."

"Whereas the men were battered and beaten. My brother was badly affected by it all – not many physical scars but the mental ones are clear enough to see. All part of the war effort."

"I saw some of that damage when I briefly did a bit of auxiliary nursing in the first war ... volunteering at Ally Pally. I wasn't trained of course so it was menial stuff, bed baths, helping with meals, washing sheets and the like. Of course, this was an internment camp, so the patients were the enemy. Trust me to choose an alternative position to the norm. We were under strict instructions not to speak to the men and in the end, I couldn't stand it."

"Never quite had you down as the nursing type," Oliver smiled. "Anyway, surely you supported the war effort as a keen suffragette?"

"We were suffragists – big difference. We took exception to all the infighting and stuck with the Fawcett side of the argument. Besides, our side of the suffrage divide decidedly rejected violent action – unlike the Pankhursts – and where we naturally felt more comfortable. Left to my own devices, I might have switched sides in time, but Dora didn't have a constitution that could manage demonstrating in the rain, and the cold, or being grappled to the ground by a police officer. So, we did very little to alter the path of history – a few banners held on a few of the meeker marches, or lending our voices of encouragement from the sidelines. We were never brave enough to lob an egg or two."

Oliver raised his eyebrows and kicked at the grass. "Seeing the effect on my brother was why I became a conchie in '38."

"Ah yes," she smiled, "a conchie ..."

"Well, a conchie, until the news came out about the death camps. I was late to the party, so they gave me a cushy number intercepting enemy morse code messages. I guess they were worried about me running for cover the minute I saw any action, so kept me well behind enemy lines, signed me up to the Royal Corps of Signalmen and stuck me in a small village in Leicestershire of all places. I sat about with a bunch of lovely girlies, doing turn-and-turn about shifts, twenty-four hours a day, and sending on what we could determine. No action – bar a feeble attempt to break a rabbit's neck on a local farm."

This was an unusually open conversation; Beatrix didn't want Oliver to stop. "Mind you it came close in the forties when you think about it. Were you at the Gateways the night we were, the one that turned out to be the first night of the Blitz? Dora and I were remembering that visit earlier and we weren't sure of it."

"No that was a particular Saturday night that I missed. I was out of town."

"Didn't put you off though did it – you carried on going in, whereas we never returned."

"Went up, every opportunity I could. You were missed you know."

"Well, we dearly missed all of it. Dora and I were recalling how safe and free a place it was for us only this morning, but in truth it was beginning to be a struggle getting her up and back on the train, as well as the cost of the tickets to the kind of things we wanted to see and do. I let her think it was the bombs and then the breaking of the habit once the war was over – but really it was all getting too much."

"I mostly stuck to the Kings' down the road – more my scene – the Gateways used to be quite a mixed crowd, but during the war it became less and less frequented by my set."

"Less prancing, more talking at the Kings, I suppose."

"Well, you and I were not the prancing types, were

we? Leaning on the bar putting the world to rights over a stiff gin-and-it was more our style. To be honest, some of those butches with their dubonnets and lemon gave me the willies."

"And me. Dora didn't mind them, she's quite attracted to extremes, but they were never my style. She got cross with me when once I called some of that behaviour showing off, but I think you know what I mean. Do you still go in often? I realise I have no idea. We have become such country folk!"

"A bit, but that whole club scene rather gets me down now. I'm too old for it. I don't want to become one of those pathetic old boys, sat in the corner, nursing a martini, ogling the boys, fancying themselves still in the game . . . or worse . . . paying for love with offers of dinner and theatre tickets and the like and then becoming bitter at being let down."

Beatrix was not sure she was entirely comfortable with this line of conversation. It not her business to know what Oliver got up to, but he was not old, and she felt it was necessary to deflect his conclusions, as a friend.

"Oliver, I won't hear you say you are past anything, you know that. Still time for *one more turn on the roundabout* as Dora would say, though the rest is none of my business."

"Thanks to you, Beatrix Veal, I will bear the roundabout in mind."

"Why did you think I wouldn't like *Sons and Lovers*?" she asked, after a pause, wanting to get them both back onto firmer ground.

"Well, I guess I thought you would think him a pathetic character who blamed everyone for his troubles — mostly his mother."

"It was rather all too obvious — but I found myself liking

both him and, in a way, his mother – which I suppose is what Lawrence wanted. Could have done without all that girding of loins though. You know, it bothered me enough to take the time to count them!"

"Interestingly obsessive on your part perhaps?" said Oliver, his twitching mouth revealing just how much he was amusing himself. "Yes, well Lawrence liked a loin. Though it is debatable whether he was keener on those of women – or men – the more."

"You don't say. I had absolutely no idea. Wait till I tell Dora."

"I'm not saying he did anything about it, but, take it from me, it's bleeding obvious in his writing."

They stood and stared at the view until she said, "Shall we go into the copse?"

"Just a minute, I want to give you something." Oliver pulled out the neatly wrapped small brown paper package from his coat pocket.

Beatrix unravelled the string that held the parcel. It was a novel; the cover of the hardback depicted a knife with three drops of blood falling from its tip. "*All That Glitters* by Primus Qualcast", she read out loud. "Why thank you, very kind," she said, turning it over to the back, wondering if this would be quite to her taste and hoping that didn't show.

"It's a galley copy – so you may find a few misprints. It's high time for me to reveal my true identify with my about-to-be-published debut."

"You . . . are Primus?"

"I am he. He's been *my nom de plume*, my alter ego, for these past fifteen years."

"He sounds very camp, if I may say so," laughed Beatrix.

"I'll tell him that you said so," said Oliver, refusing to allow Primus in on the conversation.

"'A real page turner from Mr Qualcast and a delight to meet his detective hero, Bertie Veal. An excellent read,' Shaun Woodville THE SUNDAY TIMES. The *Sunday Times*, no less," said Beatrix, reading the back cover.

"Sorry about the name. You don't mind, do you?" said Oliver, looking at her with his head on one side.

"Not at all, I'm flattered. Very flattered," said Beatrix, stroking the cover, as if it were pure velvet, the touch of it penetrating through her gloves. "Very kind of you indeed to give me this. I wonder now I look at this if I might have read any of Primus's short stories in the magazines in the shop ... how funny!"

"Yes, indeed you may. This is hot-off-the-press, it won't be in the shops for a while yet," said Oliver, smiling. "I expect they pay people to read it and give it a good review you know ..."

"Really? Well, I never."

"Sorry, only teasing. I am glad you are pleased; I was worried ... I mean that you would think the lesser of me ... that's why I never told you I was Primus. I mean detective stories are not your thing at all."

"There's always hope," she said, and thought, now is the time, now is the time.

"Oliver, I ..."

"... actually ... I have given you this today for a reason. I need to tell you something," he said, interrupting her.

"Ah," she said. "So do I ... tell you something ... and ask you something as well, but mine can wait. You go first."

"Beatrix, I hope you will forgive me ... what am I saying ... I know you will forgive me, because gently and politely you have been skilfully encouraging me not to lose myself here. However happy these past years have been, you have been right – they can't be the be-all and end-all of my life, so ... I have ... I have accepted an offer to move to Canterbury ... not an impossible distance ... and I will come, find a way to make sure I come and see you, but there you have it – I am leaving in a few weeks."

"Ah I see ... Oliver I ..."

"I know I should have said something before – about the idea of the plan, but in truth I wanted to be absolutely sure it was going to happen ... that I wanted it to happen I mean ... and it seemed unkind to test it out on you in advance of my knowing and put you through the thought of my leaving, when it might not have been the case. And anyway, who am I to say, to be vain enough to say, that it would have mattered to you as much as I feared."

"Oliver, stop it. You must not tangle yourself up so; you are as bad as me. I am delighted, truly delighted and for reasons of my own – as well as for you. It's wonderful. The book and the move. Where are you going and what are you doing?"

"You probably don't recall, as I may only have mentioned them in passing, but I have a cousin who runs a professional orchard near Canterbury. It's very seasonal, but they also have a small farm of dairy cows that provide a year-round income. It's not a huge place, but it is a going concern. They have asked me to go and stay before; it really is a beautiful place, Kent. They are getting on a bit, and they have decided to find someone to learn the business with a view to taking it over when they retire – they have no children, or any other relative who wants to have anything to do with the place. They've asked me if I would be interested in living there and helping out, learning the business and taking the strain, in return for it all becoming mine on their death. It's an unusual idea, but then they are unusual people. There is a cottage on the land that would be perfect for me.

It has quite a big kitchen garden that has fallen behind and needs looking after apparently – you will have to tell me everything that I need to do there – I have absolutely no idea ... come and stay – show me the ropes."

Beatrix smiled. "We would be happy to."

"Though the idea of living on a farm has never been in my wildest imagination, my brother has started to push about selling this place and releasing the capital. They are right that the farm, combined with half of the flat, would give me a hell of a nest egg when they are gone. It's kind of them, but I know what you are going to say ... hardly the bright lights and nothing like Chelsea and the Gateways, or the Kings Head to hang out in, yet in truth this is about my only option. Once the flat is sold ... I will need to find a new home. Though I can feed, clothe, and warm myself from Primus's bits and pieces from his short stories in the magazines, I really can't manage any rent, and I certainly don't have the capital to buy somewhere. Seems like the best option. I do hope you agree?"

So that was it. A leaving gift. Time for both truths to surface. "Of course I do and there is a double reason for that. You see, Dora and I are also to quit this place."

"Well, now I'm blowed. I had you here forever. Why?"

"As did we. Forgive me for the short version of the tale, but the full version is painful to recount, and I have already done it once today. Suffice to say we are in debt to the bank to the point where we have to leave. The bailiffs come tomorrow; it has become impossible for us to stay. I never told you all our troubles, I suspect out of misguided self-regard. I fooled myself that I could sort it so you would never need to know. I also didn't want to worry you about our leaving ... what foolish souls we are ... caring so much about our pride we denied ourselves the support we should have taken. But there it is, you are for the new road, Dora and I are for the high road."

"I didn't have an inkling that it had become so tough. Where will you go?"

"To my sister's in Durham, though that's not as simple as it may sound."

"In truth I don't recall you ever mentioning you had a sister."

"You don't say. Well, that says it all. It will be only for a short time ... then something else will come along." She tried to sound sure, solid. Reassure him there was a plan.

"Well ... that would be good. It's very important to me that you are OK. So ... we both are on to Lord knows what next, how odd. Even more reason to keep in touch, make sure you're both all right."

Though he must have been brim full of questions, he took the steer from her manner and shut it down, far too polite to press on any account if she did not wish it. This was Oliver.

"I am sorry Oliver. I don't want to be rude ... about not talking further I mean ... about the details of the how, and the why and when it all went so wrong, I am sure you understand it's painful."

"No, no, quite, quite," he said, picking up a large stick and peeling off the small twigs to make it into a reasonable walking aid, or weapon. Satisfied with the look of it he strode about, trying it out for size.

"Well, it is all sorted now, in a manner of speaking, and we are heading to Durham with all the ghastliness there that awaits us. Dora wants to do a flit first thing in the morning and not face the music. She may well be right and that's the best way."

"I tend to agree with her. Why put yourself though all

that. In fact," he said, standing still, ". . . in fact, now it comes to me . . . I can do something for you if you will let me. No one wants a tearful scene, but someone must let them in, or there will be a storming of the shop that will be talked of for years to come. You don't want that as the end of the story. Let me be there for you."

"No, Oliver. Why should you suffer those ghastly men?"

"Well, someone has to . . ."

Beatrix could see the sense in this. "I tell you what . . . we will leave the keys to the shop and the front door in the wash-house. I suspect our landlord's little side-kick, Miss Moyle, will have been instructed to come and she will arrive about half past eight, we will be long gone by then. You can give her the keys and that way she must wait for the bailiffs herself, and you can be shot of the scene."

"Consider it done," he said, smiling gently, which cheered her, and leading her into the shade of the copse by walking ahead whilst pushing and prodding at things with the stick. This was the moment, she thought, now for the letter.

"In fact, there is something else you do need to know."

"Fire away," he said, turning round.

"I am sorry, this is all coming out in a rush, and I fear you will be shocked at it but here goes. Dora and I, well perhaps in the actual pecking order of desire, I and then Dora, came to a rather terrible conclusion a few weeks ago that we would, we would take a rather drastic action, it might appear to others, but an action that had become totally rational from our point of view to . . . to . . . well to put it baldly . . . to end our lives."

"Dear Lord, what are you talking about – how had it come to that?"

"Well . . . believe me . . . in the talking about it now, it feels as if I am talking about another person, another couple entirely, but it felt to me and then gradually to both of us that ... rather than face the music we would drift off and not have to deal with ... with all the shame and all the upset and the difficulties we were to face. After all Dora and I are both in the autumn of our days. Oliver don't look at me like that."

"I'm sorry. No criticism intended by my looks. It's just so upsetting and the way you are talking about it, as though it were so ... well ... so normal and an everyday kind of a thing to think."

"That is how it was. You will notice I am saying how it WAS because we have changed our minds. It was a stupid gesture, a victory finger up to the world you might say, but we neither have the will, nor the desire come to that, to follow it through. In truth it got us through the days leading up to today because, having come to the decision and worked out a plan of how, we didn't need to think further about it. There we are. We are doing a flit and we are not going to do anything ... as folks would say, though I might dispute it ... foolish."

"Well, thank God for that."

"However, the fact is that before we decided to change the plan ... this morning as it so happens ... I posted you a letter. A letter, which I am now very sorry to say will arrive tomorrow morning."

"I see."

Beatrix could see from Oliver's expression that this revelation had made him painfully aware just how close things had come. His reaction stopped her from denying to herself how dreadful everything had been. She pushed on, sticking to her prepared script.

"It really is very factual – don't worry, it contains no

great revelation. It is a request for you to come to the shop and, I am sorry to say now, find us, and deal with all the issues that would arise. Some of which still pertain – like the hens. I suggest taking them to Greengage's where they will end their days. None of them have names . . ." She felt the tears rising.

"Well, that is a relief. I would hate to get them upset by calling them the wrong ones!" He allowed himself a nervous laugh before stopping and taking her hand briefly. "Dearest Beatrix, this is such a shocking conversation for me to assimilate – but I am touched beyond anything that you would write and ask me to be the one."

Beatrix could see, as she knew he would, that Oliver had taken on board in an instant all that would follow, all that would be publicly conveyed in their death, how badly things might be done if he were not there to protect their memory and their love for each other with dignity, how vital he would be in making all be well, because he understood why their life had been kept so hidden.

"I am very proud that you thought to ask me," he said, looking serious and deep into her eyes which wasn't usual for either of them. "I am only cross with myself that I had not realised how bad things were for you. I don't know, but I guess I never thought about the finances, even though of course I could tell that the shop was a shadow of its former self. Stupid of me and I should have."

"Well," said Beatrix, holding back her tears as best she could, "there you are then. A silly letter is going to arrive, and I would ask that you rip it up. Don't read it, please Oliver, for my sake, just tear it up – or burn it on your paraffin stove – or anything – just promise me that."

"Of course, I will, I won't let you down. I promise." Then after a pause. "Dear me, what a pickle you have been in – and what a good act you have made of not showing it. What you have been through I can't imagine ... we will both make sure this isn't goodbye, won't we?"

"Of course we will. Dora explicitly wanted me to say that to you. We'll meet again. Lord, is it just me or do you also think Vera Lynn murdered the phrase with that song? Perhaps not her fault, but it rendered it useless. Of course, we will see each other again."

"Don't know where ... don't know when ..." he sang, with his arms flung wide, she knew to break the mood however hard that was.

"Don't get old Oliver, just promise me that," she said, and so, not wanting to have to face up to any more of her own shortcomings, she walked out of the copse to the daylight.

Chapter Six

Beatrix let herself in through the front door and hung up her coat and hat. All was quiet – Dora must still be asleep. She placed Oliver's book on the table, then picked it up and opened the flyleaf. She breathed in the slightly sweet aroma of printer's ink. She was tempted to sit and read the first chapter, but she should really get on with the many tasks in hand. What a thing to tell Dora when she finally surfaced. She satisfied herself with a peek at the title page and was amazed to see written there, *To my friend Beatrix Veal*. It touched her deeply to know that he valued her enough to make such a public proclamation.

The scullery felt surprisingly chilly. She opened the stove door to find white ashes had formed a thick, deadening crust; the forgotten fire was starved. In the hurly-burly of the day the warm heart of the house had been neglected. She poked the pile – a few amber veins glowed, sucking at the air, but nothing much. Damn it, she would have to start again from scratch.

She knelt on the hearth, shut the stove door, and pulled the metal side lever up and down – a harsh riddle that would bring in the oxygen, but sadly put pay to the rest of the lit coals. She opened the kindling store cupboard on the side and piled in the sticks she had collected over the past months from the garden and the lanes; she ripped, twisted, and knotted some pages from Dora's discarded copies of the local rag. The coal was nearly out in the bucket but that was helpful – she would start with these small pieces and coax a revival. Remaining on her knees, she watched as a thin blue flame began to creep from her lit match along the edges of the newspaper and smiled as the slenderest of the sticks began to pulse with a feeble yellow glow. She encouraged the embers with a gentle blow and as soon it was getting going, she shut the stove door – the more to increase the draft.

Rising and rubbing the stiffness away from her knees she remembered that she'd had nothing to eat since breakfast. That was the way with her – she never felt hungry, just bad tempered, or alternatively tired. Food was fuel; not much to be considered otherwise and often therefore forgotten. Dora loved her meals, looked forward to them even, despite her often-referred-to acidity, though she was a slow eater. Beatrix would be sitting at the table, the clock ticking onwards, the day hastening – desperate to get on with something, or to switch on the evening's radio programme but waiting, waiting for Dora to finish chewing her food. Always a talker, having food on her plate seemed to stimulate Dora's need to communicate, despite a mouth full of corned beef, peas and mashed potato.

Dora had also not yet eaten, so Beatrix considered what they should have. She recalled suggesting an eggy something for lunch – *Nöel Coward's favourite*, Dora called it. Yes, that would do - the stove might manage that in short order. She could take Dora up a little eggy something on a tray. The meter in the hall ticked rapidly and then clunked shut. The end of the gas. Dora must have left the fire turned full on to get through that lot; she'd better go upstairs and turn it off before she put any more coins in – the last thing they needed was an explosion.

The room was dark and, unlike the rest of the house, cosy; the thick curtains drawn. She pulled them back and moved across to the fireplace to turn off the valve. She went to the foot of the bed and recited the Coward lyrics that they both knew so well . . .

> *Some ageing ladies with a groan*
> *Renounce all beauty lotions,*
> *They dab their brows with Eau de Cologne*
> *And turn to their devotions,*
> *We face the process of decay*
> *Attired in a negligée*
> *And with hot bottles at our toes*
> *We cosily in bed repose*
> *Enjoying, in a rather languid way,*
> *A little eggy something on a tray.*

"How's about it?" Beatrix said. Then rather louder, prodding at Dora's feet deep beneath the eiderdown, "Come on, duckie, shake-a-leg. We have discussions to be had, decisions to be made and work to do. I don't suppose you heard the telephone even if Alice did call?"

She moved round to Dora's side of the bed, pulled back the covers and put her hand onto Dora's round shoulder to give it a shake. As soon as she touched her, she felt the absence.

"Dora? Dora? Wake up. Come on . . ." and she shook her again, as if this nudging, this calling, would bring her back from where she had gone.

"Oh, Dora, Dora, what have you gone and done?" she said, sinking to her knees beside the bed. "No. Oh no ... Dora ... please ... come on, please ..." – as if this would be the reminder Dora needed – the reminder of her duty to live. She touched the shoulder again; it felt the same – an absolute failure to respond. She put her finger to Dora's open mouth. No breath, slack-mouthed. Gone.

She pulled back the eiderdown and blankets even further. She pulled hard at the sheet that was wrapped under Dora, freeing the dead weight from the clinging starched cotton. She took in the, oh so, familiar clothes, hair, hands, the shape in the world that was Dora, though not the same.

She was lying exactly as she slept; on her side, facing the edge of the bed, her legs bent as if kneeling, her hands together as if in prayer and tucked up under her cheek.

Her normally mobile face was composed, still. Her eyes closed, her skin pallid, slowly solidifying like cooling wax. She had, thank-the-Lord, removed her makeup and was – though she would not be happy about it – *au naturelle*. Her teeth – she would be happy about this – were in. The smeary glasses were folded and on the bedside table, the aunt's signet ring, the brooch they bought together in Hastings, her mother's pearl necklace and jade earrings would be lying redundant in the dish on the dressing table close by.

"Christ, Dora. What happened, what on earth has just happened to you? – and to me?"

Beatrix sat back on her haunches on the mat, stroking the bedding, stroking her own hair, touching, touching everything, but Dora. She feared another touch of that still soft body, feared, in its certainty, the absolute departure of everything that was Dora; of everything that was a future with Dora.

The phone began to ring. She counted the number of double tones, seven-eight, nine-ten, eleven-twelve, thirteen-fourteen. How many times before it fell silent? No talking to people now, especially not to Alice. She probably wasn't invited to Durham with Dora, and she would never ever go there without her . . . twenty-seven, twenty-eight . . . silence.

She stood up and covered Dora with the eiderdown. The room was cooling. Perhaps she should let it – in its new role as morgue? How long till rigor mortis? How long till decomposition? How long did she have here alone with Dora? She didn't want anyone else to come – ever. She moved slowly to the chair; her legs leaden – *all the stuffing knocked out of her* as Dora would say. She looked at her watch – twenty-past two. What to do? What was the right thing to be done? She looked back repeatedly to the bed and then away again, as if on the returning fearful glance things would be changed. On one of the returns her eyes stayed, glued, observing the still lump on the bed. Sitting, this far away, it was just possible she had been mistaken. What if Dora were still clinging on to life by a thread? Why hadn't she done something straight away to try to revive her? Why had she just accepted that she was dead?

She ran to the bed and turned Dora onto her back. The resistance was absolute. She wasn't stiff, but she was in no way helping. She picked up Dora's head and shook it.

"Dora. Dora, can you hear me? Can you hear me?"

She lay the head back down and peered intently at the mouth. What did she hope for? – a gurgle or a hiss of breath? Silence. She kissed the almost flabby lips. She blew into the mouth. She covered the mouth with her lips and blew into the lungs. There was a taste of vomit, but there was nothing else from Dora. Nothing. What would Dora say to do?

Phone the bally doctor you fool.

Beatrix ran down the stairs to the telephone. She looked up the number in the phone book, her fingers tracing down the small lines of names and numbers; known off-by-heart to Dora, but not to her.

"Doctor Cohen's residence?"

Almost bent double with anxiety, she leaned over the small table. "Oh, Mrs Cohen, It's Miss Veal. I wondered if Doctor Cohen were with you. I am fearful that something terrible has happened to Dora. To Dora ..." now the tears flowed, the air gulped in, as if sucked out of her. "...Terrible to Dora. I think ... I think ..."

"Hello my dear. I am so sorry, Doctor Cohen is out on his rounds, but he is expected back soon. I am sure he will come round straight away, the minute he gets back. How is she now, did you say?"

"I've just found her ... well a few minutes ago ... I think in all honesty she is dead."

"Had she fallen?"

"No. She is on our ... her ... her bed." Steady on ... steady on ... Beatrix pulled herself up to a standing position. "She was in bed having a rest and I went out for a walk, not long really, and I've come back, and I've just found her, and I don't know, I don't know ..."

"I am so sorry. He will be round just as quick as he can. Is there anyone who can sit with you whilst you wait?"

"I don't know. I don't want to ... I don't know ... I think. No, I am all right on my own, no, better on my own. Thank you. Thank you for asking." Beatrix wiped her streaming nose and eyes with the back of her hand, her sleeve ... where the hell was her hanky? She kept patting her jacket pocket then back to her face.

"Well ... if you are sure. I can easily send our Enid

over to you, I would hate for you to be on your own. I will send Doctor Cohen straight over just as soon as he comes home."

"It's so kind. Don't send Enid. I don't know ... I will, I think, see how I am. I will call you if I need her. Don't send her on my account. Don't. Thank you, thank you. Most kind of you to offer ..."

Beatrix sank down into the straight-backed hall chair, the receiver in her lap. The snot and the tears running at will. They slid onto her blouse and dropped onto her skirt. She should go back upstairs and sit with Dora, but she feared what she might find. Why? What was happening to her? She was losing her mind. It was shock, that was all, shock. Her rational mind. She never had any fear of the dead, of the living dead walking, of graveyards, or messages from the past, she scoffed at healers and soothsayers and mediums, she had never feared the dark. Dora loved all that claptrap – she even took Beatrix to see a medium once to find out their fortune. Beatrix found the whole experience discombobulating and ran as fast as she could from it, or from any further reference to it ... but Dora had no fear of crazy people. She found them amusing, whereas Beatrix found them malign – no, not that – impossibly unpredictable. She made to stand but fear stopped her from moving. What was it she feared? That Dora had become something unimaginable upstairs? This was ridiculous. Why could she not return to the bedroom and be with her? She could not be left alone up there to wait for Doctor Cohen. She put the receiver back on the rocker and the phone rang immediately. Startled she picked up the receiver, hesitated and then dropped it back on the hook. Doctor Cohen wouldn't telephone. He would come.

She sat tight in the hall waiting for her rational mind to

return to her. The house felt bereft, adrift from its usual mooring. Was Dora at peace, or only on her way to being at rest? Only Dora knew. They held two very different visions of death – Beatrix's was altogether quieter and finite. Once the soul had left the body there was nothing. She couldn't ever explain what she meant by the soul; life force didn't quite cut it, but she knew it was within every living creature and after death it was extinguished. Once gone there was no way to send a message back to base – no mind with which to formulate a thought, no voice to speak – if you were nothing in nothing; Beatrix faced the lonely future of a committed atheist. Dora the agnostic had many options to play with in life beyond death. The ones Beatrix enjoyed the most were the imaginary conversations with St Peter; poor man; Beatrix hoped he was ready for the onslaught. Mind you, Dora would not be the first agnostic to turn up with a point of view on the short comings of . . .

The Lord God Almighty. I mean . . . why bother to exist at all if He won't do anything to help the meek and defy the evil in the world? Why kill innocent children in earthquakes and floods and droughts?

Dora's voice so clear – so present.

"Well, if you believe God exists then you must believe God can't die – it kind of goes with the job, doesn't it? And as He can't resolve man's foolishness, He is stuck watching us screw it all up, over and over again. A penance for creating us in the first place. Nothing He can do but watch poor thing. I don't think our fate is God's will – I think it is God's impotence."

It is just typical of you to take sides with a deity you don't think exists.

"Just as insane to want to argue with it surely."

It? Tres modern Madam Veal.

"Dora, you had better show me a sign when you get there – if you still exist that is."

Don't you worry duckie, believe me if there is anything there I will. Though it means you will have to apologise to the vicar and live a pious life to the end – so maybe I better had not!

She was being cruel by staying downstairs. Perhaps it would be impossible for Dora's soul to leave her body, left upstairs as she was on her own. She'd better go back up.

As Beatrix reached the door, her fear returned. A monster was lurking on the other side – a huge grey screaming blob-of-a mass – that would suck her into its gooey mouth, drag the lifeblood out of her. Why fear it? It was of no matter; she was happy to meet her fate. She turned the handle. The silence in the room beat on her eardrums; the life force outside the room was utterly different from that within. She crept back in, not wanting to disrupt the powerful vacuum that Dora's death had created. Dead quiet.

Standing at the foot of the bed, Beatrix knew she had to try to hold on to the parts of Dora that remained; slipping away without being captured for the last time was not an option. She kneeled on the mat beside Dora, leaned across and breathed in deeply over the crown of Dora's head. There, holding fast for now, was that unmissable aroma of Johnson's baby shampoo, Vosene hairspray, and 4711 Original Eau de Cologne – her trademark. The turquoise-and-gold bottle, a fresh supply given each Christmas day and received with grace, was winking at her from the dressing table. Maybe she would take up wearing it in her grief? Maybe.

She walked to the dressing table and began trying on Dora's jewellery; first the aunt's signet ring, which Dora wore on her little finger, slipped comfortably onto Beatrix's middle one. Next the string of pearls round her neck – how many times had she helped to *fix these for me darling, won't you?* Then the brooch to the neck of her blouse as Dora would wear it. Lastly, in turn, she screwed on the dangly jet earrings to her earlobes. My goodness they were uncomfortable, how did Dora bear them? She opened a drawer and took out a fresh lace hanky, took off her jacket and picked up the favourite mauve cashmere cardigan that was always left hanging over the back of the chair when Dora undressed. She exchanged its resting place with her jacket and slid her arms along the plump sleeves that ended too soon. She looked in the dressing table mirror. The garment hung on her like a new-born piglet's skin whose body was wanting to grow. She dabbed the Eau de Cologne onto the hanky, behind her ear and onto her wrists, a wretched doppelganger's still-living pulse points. She popped open the cardboard pot and stroked blusher on her cheeks before drawing her thin lips together with sticky dark Red Velvet lipstick. She opened the glass powder jar, the large soft powder-puff breathed a cloud of Pink Champagne – the unmistakable waft of Helena Rubinstein, that alluring, floral aroma that signalled show time, filling the room as she puffed her cheeks. Beatrix stepped back, observed herself and removed the earrings. Too far.

She sat on the end of the bed at Dora's feet. What a pile of bloody messed up mess she was left with to face alone. All their promises and pacts all dumped in a flash – and she out for a damn walk. Not here. Had Dora called out? Had she realised what was happening? What had happened exactly? How frightened had she been? How had she behaved as she went up the stairs when Beatrix left for her walk? – a bit wan, a bit, *ah me I feel a little wobbly*, but that was said on so many, many days by Dora. Had she been selfish not to realise that this was in some way leading to something more? Well, thank you – absent God – another perfect demonstration of impotence on your part. Timing is all. Why now? Why today? Couldn't this have waited just a little, for another damn day? Unless – could it be that Dora had broken the deal and, in some way, taken action into her own hands? She looked so peaceful lying there – too peaceful perhaps? She looked exactly as if she had fallen into a deep sleep. Beatrix turned and opened the drawer of Dora's bedside table. *Doctor Cohen's bottles of tricks*, Dora called them. She was sure the way Dora told it was in fact the case, that Doctor Cohen was an innocent in the subterfuge that Dora had worked for many years as he over-prescribed this and over-prescribed that. Yet, as she was never allowed to accompany Dora to the doctor's house how could she know? Dora was careful never to overplay the deceit as she stashed away little brown bottles of pills for a rainy day that never came, and so the drawer grew full. Quite what this was all about was beyond Beatrix. This doctor–patient power game in which Dora took great delight in out-foxing the gentleman and getting more than her fair share of his sweeties. Sleeping pills, calmers, uppers, painkillers, tubes of mysterious creams and bottles of soothing lotions – or laxatives. This bedside table alone had enough supply of pills for a hypochondriac to survive for at least six months, without a repeat prescription.

You just never know, darling. One day you will thank me – you wait and see how much you need Doctor Cohen's bottles of tricks to hove in to view.

And, of course, it had come true as the plot developed for them to end their days at their own hands. Dora had enough sleeping pills to kill half the village.

*

Beatrix opened the drawer. How would she be able to tell if a bottle, or more, had gone down Dora's neck? She would have had plenty of time to swill them down and neatly shut the drawer. There was no evidence of an empty bottle on the bedside table, no water glass discarded on the floor. Besides, in the dark days when they had discussed this, Dora was determined they should dissolve the pills in hot milk before adding sugar. She was adamant on this point, though Beatrix never understood why. She supposed she had read it in one of her magazines, though somehow that seemed an unlikely topic for *Woman's Realm* or *Women's World*. THIS WEEK IN OUR HEALTH SECTION, IMOGEN BATELY ADVISES 'How to take your life in five easy steps.' 1) First warm the milk. 2) Add three spoons of sugar, to taste. 3) Crush the sleeping pills – make sure enough ... Beatrix shut the drawer – impossible to tell.

The phone rang in the hall. She moved to the chair by the window and counted them again: twenty-seven ... twenty-eight ... twenty-nine ... she let it ring until it stopped. Telling Alice that Dora was dead would lead to a host of questions she could not answer. How did it happen? What was next? What now for Beatrix? Did this change anything? Then there would be the silence down the line – waiting for her to meet the obligation to invite them to the funeral, that gesture laced with the knowledge that they would so much rather not have to come.

The funeral. Dora had been very precise on the guest list and slippery on the disposal of her mortal remains. The guest list was made up of obligations and a handful of friends. She had spent some time working on it as if organising a dinner party.

I am worried if you invite Betsy, she won't know a soul.

Or:

I think you had better invite Henrietta and Tim after all – as they know the Burbages and they won't have anyone to talk to otherwise.

But as time went on the list became shorter and shorter – Vera had followed Mary and pretty much all the others were gone. All the good-time show girlies that passed the time so well in the twenties and thirties had faded into the mist as soon as Dora proved herself too old to keep up with the crowd. The Burbages, a local couple who had been friendly when they first arrived in the village, were in fact still living, but they had lost touch through having so little in common; she could see them opening the invitation and wondering how to refuse. Who would be there? Oliver certainly, the vicar and his wife, and, she supposed, Mr and Mrs Hodge plus of course William. Some of the other customers out of a sense of duty? The thought of it made her skin creep. She wondered if she could just do it alone with the vicar and stick her in the ground – which was as close as Dora got to explaining her thoughts.

Beatrix wanted to be . . .

Burned and scattered to the four winds in a park in Chelsea. Yes, I've got that darling. Now, be sure to order enough food for mine – and for goodness' sake make sure there's both sweet and dry sherry. I know what you are like and won't think of it, but funerals are exhausting, and everyone needs a sherry when they arrive at the wake. The brandy goes straight into the bloodstream you know, that's why it's so good for a faint – and then they will need hot food (not ruddy fish paste sandwiches curling at the edge) to soak it all up.

Sod the hot food, that was going too far. Beatrix wondered if she would still be able to invite whoever came back here after the funeral. She would splash out on two bottles of sherry. Dora liked a Bristol Cream. How much did a funeral cost? What if she couldn't scrape together enough money? Was there such a thing as a pauper's burial, a pauper's grave anymore? And if so, what was it and where would it be? There was much to do, so much unknown, and much she feared. Her capable strong hands, which had always opened everything, were heavy in her lap. The blue veins were flowing automatically, requiring no attention from her; but everything else did. She was brain-achingly tired; drained of any willpower. Dora's absence had bleached her clean of any motivation – no, worse – any need – to continue being the one who solved, sorted, fixed.

It's too late in the movie of your life to change your casting now darling.

"Very droll, Dora – and bugger off," she muttered over her shoulder.

Then again, what did that matter anymore? Here they both were and nothing more was needed. All was said and done – by Dora, by Beatrix, or by anyone else who might have taken a view. She no longer needed to hear it. The buzz of the cars on the arterial road droned on, the heeled shoes tripped on by beneath her window. Innocents driving themselves onward to find a motive for living, or strolling down a pavement for a purpose: a wedding to get to, a letter to post, a pregnancy to discover, an assignment to fluster over, a lover to find. In here, in their bedroom, the future had stopped.

Loud, urgent, knocking on the front door below broke into their peaceful place, far worse than the telephone – that could be ignored. It was so reminiscent of the hammering that had woken her that lifetime ago this morning, that she thought it must be William returned at the end of the day, even though she had told him not to come. She couldn't face opening the door to William. Though goodness knows that moment of opening the door to someone would have to be endured soon, unless she found a way to escape it. Or perhaps Terry had returned home and now was come to demand the keys again – she definitely would not open up for that.

The banging continued as Beatrix sat, her hands in her lap unmoved. No, she would not open up for anyone ... unless ... of course, how stupid of her, it was Doctor Cohen, come at last. Though she knew there was no hope, the arrival of the doctor, a professional death person, who could explain what's what – what might have occurred, the cause – brought an unexpected flood of relief. The hammering continued. A strange way for a doctor to arrive at the house of the dead. But there it was, she was grateful for his urgency.

She tore down the stairs and ran to the front door, to find, not Doctor Cohen, but Oliver on the doorstep.

"Oh, thank goodness," he said. "For a moment I thought ... I thought ... well I thought ... that despite what you had said about changing your minds ... something terrible had happened. I have been calling you since just after I got back to my flat from our walk, didn't you hear the telephone? You picked up once – but the line went dead. I have had some incredible news and I wanted to let you know ... I've been calling you. Why, Beatrix, whatever is the matter?"

"I thought the phone was Alice."

"Why didn't you answer?"

"I'm sorry, Oliver, I can't talk now – I am waiting for Doctor Cohen."

"Has something happened? Beatrix, you're looking very

odd. Can I come in?" And with that he pushed the front door wide and moved her back into the dark hall. She stood stock-still, guarding the bottom of the stairs.

"I don't think you should be here Oliver – not until the Doctor comes. Dora has ... Dora is ... she is in the bedroom now. I think she has had some sort of terrible fit – or something – in her sleep, whilst I was with you. She's upstairs now. She's ... not breathing, not breathing – not any breath at all. I can't find any breath in her."

"My goodness, Beatrix. You poor thing. Shall we go upstairs and ..."

"No. No thank you. I don't want her disturbed. I don't want that ..." Beatrix was feeling the need to raise her voice. Why wouldn't the wretched man just leave her to wait for the professional? She didn't want any intrusion.

"Then let us go and sit down together and wait for Doctor Cohen, you can't be alone, really you can't. I am not leaving you like this."

Beatrix led the way to the scullery. She sat down at the little table. She could think of nothing to say. Perhaps it was acceptable that Oliver was here, but she was totally unsure what to do with him now that he was.

"Shall I make you some tea?" he asked.

"No. No thank you. Anyway, I think the stove must've gone out by now, it's been neglected, what with one thing and another. It doesn't matter." It had been a catastrophic day; one in which she had ricocheted through a series of events that piled one on top of the other. Each had felt like the worst thing at the time yet now seemed utterly irrelevant. "You really can go; I will be fine."

"What time did you call the doctor?" Oliver asked, ignoring her, and filling the kettle. What a stupid question, but she supposed it was his plan – to keep her talking. The

kettle filled, he put it on the stove. He opened the door –
she looked over her shoulder. The glow of a fire was there.

"See, Beatrix, it's alive. Don't worry." He fed in some
sticks and the remains of the coal in the scuttle and the flame
rose; the coals warmed.

"Nothing worse than a cold stove – well perhaps a cold
body." She shrugged her shoulders, stroked her mouth, and
rubbed her face; she rubbed the palm of her hand up and
over her mouth and nose. It felt comforting to feel her own
face. Warming.

The clock ticked; time wasted. Where was that dratted
doctor?

"Did I say I'm waiting for Doctor Cohen?"

"Yes. Yes, you did. How long has it been?" he said,
slipping off his hat and coat. He kept the muffler on; she
supposed he was right it was chilly in here. She pulled
Dora's cardigan close.

"I have no idea. You can go when he comes ... I will
have to help him, I am sure."

"Did you find her straight away when you came back? It
must have been the most terrible shock."

"I don't know, it took a while. I was going up to ask her
if she wanted an egg for her lunch and there she was. On
the bed, gone. Or at least I think she has gone. I shook her,
not hard, not enough to hurt her, just to wake her. I tried
to give her the kiss-of-life – but nothing. I mean it seems
clear that she's dead, but how do you truly know? I guess
that's why you call the doctor."

"Oh, I think you know."

Beatrix sat back in her chair and looked at Oliver, "You
seem very sure about that," she said.

"Well, I have seen a dead person before ... a couple in
fact, I am sorry to say."

"A couple? Do you mean together?"

"Would you like me to go and check, make sure that you are correct? I mean I am sure you are – but if you would like me to check then I will," he said, ignoring her.

"When did you see a dead body?"

"Now is not the time for that. Do you want me to go up? You don't have to come with me."

"I don't know. I don't really want anyone else to see her like that. I'm not sure she would wish it. In fact, I know she would hate it. She hasn't got any of her makeup on."

"Unlike you."

"Sorry?"

"Well, to be blunt, you don't look quite your normal self."

"I must look totally deranged," said Beatrix, getting up from her chair quickly. As she did, she began to stumble and clutched at the oilcloth on the table.

"Steady, steady on . . . you are nearly in a faint and hardly surprising. Beatrix, sit. Please, please sit down, and let me bring you whatever you need. I am sorry I shouldn't have told you about your face – but with the doctor coming I thought you would want to know. It has rather smudged around your mouth and eyes, in a way I am not sure you originally intended."

"Thank you for not laughing at me."

"Why on earth would I laugh at you?"

"I must look like an old strumpet."

"More like a pantomime dame gone a bit astray, if I am brutally honest."

Beatrix started to laugh – why not? What else mattered? She dropped her head in her hands on the table to hide her face.

"What is to become of me now, Oliver? What in hell's

name is to become of me now?" She was aware of her quickening breath, her heart – a racing beat; she began to pant. She had seen this enough in Dora – the drowning woman – and now she did not know how to talk herself back up to the surface and the air. There wasn't enough air in the room.

"Hey, hey, slow down. We need to talk much more about that, but first there is tea, then there is your face to sort, then Doctor Cohen to face, then next and next and next . . . but first there is calmer slower breathing, in and out . . . and in and out . . . just think about that and nothing more . . . please, just for a while? You need to become calm." He took her hands in his and it was indeed calming, no inner tremor, no faint heart, so different to Dora's.

The kettle began to steam. Oliver rose and warmed the brown pot, swilling out the water into the sink. He found the tea, spooned the leaves into the pot and poured in the boiling water. He found the cups and saucers, he found the milk bottle in the pantry, he found the sugar bowl.

"I don't take sugar, thank you," she said, her head still resting on her arms on the table, aware of the purpose in all his single-handed movements; she knew the room so well. She heard the pouring and the stirring.

"You do now. Doctor Cohen would not forgive me otherwise," he said, placing the cup and saucer beside her arm. She could feel the warmth from it; *the life's blood*, as her father would have said. For a doctor, he had a highly questionable faith in the healing properties found within a cup of tea.

Beatrix sat up and sipped, under orders. She ran her tongue around her teeth, wondering if those were as smeared in the goo of Red Velvet as her face. Just like some of those old dykes at the Gateways whose grinning faces leered at the younger, fresher meat, as it arrived on a Saturday night.

She ran the back of her hand over her lips. Yes, a quantity of lipstick was still there, smearing her mottled skin.

"OK, now you are just making it worse. Where is your cold cream?" he said.

"How do you know about a thing like cold cream, Oliver?"

"I had a mother you know – the wife of a vicar uses cold cream – just like everyone else," he smiled.

"You never said your father was a vicar?"

"Would it have made a difference?"

"No of course not, but it makes me realise I didn't know you had a faith, which I must suppose you do. Is it too shocking to reveal that I am an atheist and Dora an agnostic?"

"I assumed as much on account of the fact I never saw either of you at the church."

"You go to church?"

"Strictly for the formal set celebrations, births, marriages and deaths, Christmas and Easter. Call it an insurance policy. I find the routine reassuring."

"What a number of debates we might have had stomping over the fields, if I had known."

"Perhaps, though I like to keep my thoughts on my own faith to myself. I find they don't respond well to scrutiny. Now where is that cold cream?"

"It's on the table in our bedroom – the front room at the top of the stairs. I don't really want you to go there though."

"Because it would upset me?"

"No. Dora."

"If Dora is dead, she is unable to be upset. Beatrix, I must go up and check. I very much fear that she is, but I will go up now and check, put your mind, and frankly my mind, at rest – find the cold cream and the cotton wool and we can fix your face."

"Well, if you are sure and think that is for the best," Beatrix said, surprised at how relieved she was; it was not her decision so any betrayal, however unlikely to ever be felt, could be blamed on Oliver.

"I won't be long – back in a tick," he said and left the room, a greyhound finally let off the leash.

Beatrix looked about the little scullery. This snug room that had been their haven from the world was now redundant. She stroked the oilcloth, running her hands along its green, waxy ridges. She picked up the two sausage-shaped white napkins held by their silver rings. French silver. Why did that sound far more exotic, so much more exclusive, than Sterling? They had their initials etched on the central disk of each ring, designed for the purpose, and had hand-stitched the same design on one corner of each of their four white damask napkins: the set in use and the one in the wash. The three letters overlapped, entwined. $\mathcal{BAV}$ and $\mathcal{DEH}$. The same initials had been embroidered onto their Cash's name tapes, each sewn on by hand to collars and waistbands, in her case sewn by herself, in Dora's by her mother, on every item of school uniform and scratched into the handle of every hockey stick.

The white napkins lay limp in her hands, folded last by Beatrix at the end of her breakfast. Dora's had remained untouched from the supper the night before: a tense, sad little meal where neither of them had spoken their true minds, or faced their realities. How many times had this soft damask been pulled from its ring, unfurled, laid on a lap and when replete with crumbs caught and drips blotted, folded, and returned? Every day since they had first used them in the Cromwell Road, till yesterday. How many meals made and eaten, the plate scraped, the scraps set aside for the hens? She lifted Dora's napkin – still rolled in its ring – to her mouth, just as Dora did at the end of every meal after returning her napkin to its ringed and folded state. Beatrix ran the rolled end over her lips, adding more Red Velvet to the previously blushed edge. She wondered if these rings and two clean napkins might have made it to the suitcase of treasures Dora talked about packing, had she lived to make the choice.

Beatrix sipped more tea; Oliver was right, the sweetness was a comfort to her. Of course, he needed to check upstairs for his own peace of mind. Sitting downstairs with her here, taking her word for it, when, after all, Dora was still alive up there but now dying from neglect, would be a terrible guilt – and no doubt a penance for him to inflict on himself later. She shouldn't expect him to just take her word for it. He would see for himself that Dora was dead and that would be an end to it. Unless Dora was still alive? Or come back to life? Like Juliet – and Oliver the friar come to save her. What was he doing up there? He wouldn't touch anything she was sure, though she didn't recall having said to him not to touch anything. Perhaps he couldn't find the cold cream. Perhaps he couldn't see that the jar with the silver lid concealed a pop-up surprise of pink and white cotton wool balls? Perhaps he was talking to Dora? Explaining to her that he had to come back down here to Beatrix with her cold cream, and why, and how funny and silly that was, and how surprised she, Beatrix, would be when he came down any minute now and told her that although Dora had appeared to be dead she was in fact just in a deep, deep sleep from which she had woken to find herself alone and couldn't locate her glasses. Again.

Dora would be surprised to find Oliver in her bedroom for sure, but once he had explained about the cold cream and the need for it, she would probably be calm and perhaps the deepness of her sleep state, the almost dead trance she had been in, would cause her mind to be slightly astray, more accepting of the unusual ... a man, though not a strange man ... in her room ...

Beatrix got up. Holding on to the table, her legs weaker than she had ever known them, she fixed her eyes on the door and headed for it. She must join them – it was crazy her being down here and them sharing a joke upstairs and all the time here she was downstairs sad and lonely, when after all she had just stepped through a kind of a gauze into another world, that wasn't absolutely the real world, and if she went upstairs now she would find that everything would be back as it should be, as it was – before she came home.

She stepped forward, her head held high, though it felt uncommonly heavy and as if it needed to drop down, downwards and indeed it was dropping quite fast now because she could not hold it up and the room was tipping, and she could not stop it and her body was falling in behind it. There was a knocking way in the distance at the front door, but she couldn't come now ... she was sorry she couldn't come ... but ... the chair went over and her hand hit the table hard and her arm hit the floor harder and she was gone.

Chapter Seven

Beatrix could hear a man's voice calling her from what sounded like the top of a very long tube that whirled slowly round and round like a vortex above her. "Miss Veal ... can you hear me, Miss Veal? This is Doctor Cohen. You've taken a tumble and ... perhaps a little more fanning please Mr Cope ... thank you. Miss Veal ...?"

She tried opening her eyes slowly. The spinning was slowing, and coming into view was an anxious bespectacled face with the grey beard of Doctor Cohen.

"Here we are now, here you are, Miss Veal. Yes, yes, I think she is coming round ... thank you so much, Mr Cope. Yes, lovely. Let's wipe her face and get her feeling and looking more herself, lovely, lovely. Gently, gently does it. There we are." She could feel cold cream and then a warm flannel wiping and smoothing her face and it was so refreshing, so calming, so kind.

"Dear me, dear me. We think you took quite a tumble – don't we, Mr Cope." Hands were feeling her arms and legs, professional judgements at play. "No bones broken, I am very pleased to see. You will be quite stiff from this, but nothing worse. Now do you think we can get you up on your feet and back in the chair? Mr Cope, if you would be so kind can you help me here?" And strong arms lifted her up and held her easily as she was turned and sat back in her chair. "Perhaps a cushion, my dear? There we go, now that is better, isn't it. All that was lost it seems was a teacup and saucer."

All that was lost? She felt her forehead; there was a very painful spot. Her plait had fallen out of its bun – wisps of hair were wild and loose. She re-pinned it as best she could, pulled her buttons straight, her skirt in line. She patted the sleeve of her blouse and was surprised to pull out one of Dora's lace hankies. Dora's cardigan seemed to be gone.

"How is Dora? What has happened to Dora?"

"My dear, Mr Cope was right to summon me in here the minute I arrived, which was pretty much, as I understand it, as you fainted. Now you are in a better place I will go upstairs and see to Miss Ham."

She wanted so much to stand and go with him – but something about his manner stopped her from even trying. He ran the tap, placed a folded cold flannel compress to her forehead and was gone.

Oliver picked up the shards of broken crockery at her feet and cleared the pieces away into the bin.

"How are you feeling now?"

"A bit better. I am sorry. How embarrassing."

"Glass of water?" He found a glass and ran the tap.

"You know I have never fainted in my life before. Swooning, Dora would call it. She had a terror of it and I saw her come close quite a few times."

"I only have the once and that was after I hit my head incredibly hard, and I do believe I actually saw stars." Oliver sat at the table and handed her the glass. "What a day," he said, pulling the muffler he was still wearing more tightly round his neck, as if he were feeling the chill, or perhaps to steady his nerves. He ran his hands through his receding auburn hair. She knew just how unsettling he would find all of this; she dearly wished she could make amends.

"Yes, sorry," said Beatrix, sipping her water. She shivered; Oliver was right.

"Would you like this?" Oliver said, taking Dora's cardigan from the back of her chair.

"It will do," she said, slipping it over her shoulders. "It's Dora's."

"You don't say," he said.

They sat in silence, waiting for Dr Cohen. The compress felt good. Acutely aware that Dora was not alone upstairs, yet unable to be with her, Beatrix began to run though the events from when she arrived home, piecing it all back together in her mind.

"Why are you here? You said you were calling? Why were you telephoning me? I thought you were Alice, so I didn't answer. I'm sorry."

"Stop being sorry, for goodness's sake. This hardly feels like the right moment to talk about it, we can talk another day."

"Well, as I have nothing else to contribute to the conversation, you might as well explain yourself whilst Doctor Cohen pulls Dora about upstairs, or whatever it is he is doing. Why is it taking so long? Should we go and see?"

"Perhaps not. Let's leave him to it. He will be determining the cause."

"You are very wise. Perhaps you have been through something like this before."

"Bit of both." He smiled. "All right so, as I am instructed to distract you with my selfish news ... when I returned from our walk, I had a phone call ... I am summoned to

141

London this evening for a drink with my agent to celebrate. The publisher says they are so pleased with the advance orders for my debut that they want to option two more to make a series. I am officially a writer of detective novels!"

"And my male alter ego is now to be serialised?"

"Yup."

"Does this change any of your plans?"

"May I come in?" said Doctor Cohen, pushing the door in a way that knocked it at the same time. Oliver rose – offering his chair. The compress now obscuring him from her, she put it aside.

"My dear, you were right. I am afraid she has gone. Nothing to be done. My suspicion is her heart finally failed on her. She would have known nothing about it. In her sleep . . . best way of all to go."

"Nothing to be done if I had got there sooner? Had been with her?"

"You must not distress yourself with that line of thought. Nothing. I have made out the cause of death certificate . . . natural causes. Much the best from an administrative point of view. Saves a great deal of fuss."

"Yes of course. So, her heart you say, but why would it suddenly fail like that?"

"Well, perhaps you didn't know, but Miss Ham had a serious condition for many years, angina. So, in the end, as she was well aware, the inevitable would happen."

"Angina? I never knew. She always said it was her stomach, an ulcer, her breathlessness caused by anxiety."

"Well, Miss Ham had many conditions . . . some of them real and some imaginary. Difficult patient to treat in many respects. She knew better than me on most issues concerning her health and indeed her treatment. A kind soul, but forceful in her way, wasn't she? It was a question of benign

142

management of her desires, and particularly her foibles. My one failure was letting her get so addicted to the sleeping pills, but for a doctor it is often a question of balance."

Beatrix thought of the bottles of tricks ... had he by any chance opened the drawer? "She never said. She never, ever, said." She fumbled up the sleeve of her blouse again for Dora's hanky.

"Well, though perhaps you felt you knew her better than most, clearly, she kept some things to herself. We all have our secrets and our reasons for keeping them. I am sorry but I should turn to more administrative matters. Could you provide me with her date of birth?"

"9th December 1877."

"Thank you. You will need to give this form to her next-of-kin so they can register the death."

Oliver moved from the sink on which he was leaning and, in a manner that she found immensely reassuring, stood beside her.

"Well ... I ... I suppose it had better be me who does that," she said, trying hard not to catch Doctor Cohen's eye.

"No living relatives?"

"None I am aware of." Why had she said that? Leaving it open – why so stupid?

"Would there be a way to make some enquiries – did she talk to you about a will at all?"

"Frequently."

"Do you by any chance know if there is one perhaps lodged with a solicitor? It might help you to trace any family members."

"No."

"I am sorry to be awkward and this is strictly none of my business, but time taken now to find an executor ... to find a relative ... will save so much potential difficulty later on."

"Doctor Cohen, you can rest assured I will take care of all Dora's affairs properly." Beatrix pushed Dora's hanky into her sleeve in a sign, she hoped, that this conversation was now drawing to an end. She did not dare stand up.

"Of course, of course. Please don't feel any criticism in what I have said, just trying to help. It's a difficult time. I have probably said too much. There we are. My sad work is done, and I should leave you to it." He placed Dora's death certificate on the table and stood. "Just one last thing – sorry, I nearly forgot. Are there any of her sleeping pills left by any chance? It will save you the bother if I take them now. They shouldn't be left lying about and ... and I don't believe you have any need of them?"

"Of course." Beatrix moved to stand despite herself.

"Don't be silly, I will go – where are they?" said Oliver, moving quickly to the door.

"In the drawer of her bedside table – the one with her glasses resting on it." Beatrix said, defeated again.

Doctor Cohen stood uncomfortably, waiting for Oliver's return. Beatrix could think of nothing to say. She raised the compress to her forehead again, though warm it protected her, as if it were a shield. To her relief he found the solution.

"How are you these days? I think I may have only seen you the once in all these years – a bad back, wasn't it?"

"Yes, it was. You have a very good memory."

"All better now? I hope that fall will not have set it off again. Come and see me if you feel any need, any need at all." He turned his hat in his hands, unsure. "I am sure you know of Underhill's in Beaconsfield? They will come and on presentation of the certificate they will take Miss Ham's remains away and await instructions for the funeral. They are a good family firm – they will come today, as soon as you wish, and they are very respectful. Very discreet, you know."

Beatrix could think of nothing to say, though the doctor's silence suggested she should. How quickly a person's body, so lived in, so loved, became the remains. The remains of Miss Ham. What would remain of Dora? She was quickly slipping away.

Doctor Cohen put on his hat, as if to reassure her that it was his desire to go. "I really am most terribly sorry, Miss Veal. Miss Ham was, I know, your dear friend and she was such a pleasure to have as a patient. Although she nearly drove my dear wife mad for appointments – I always felt the happier for seeing her. She was someone who held such a wise view on our human shortcomings."

"Here you are, Doctor, this is all of them." Oliver returned with a clutch of small brown bottles, each with a carefully hand-written label, which he passed to the doctor. "More here than I thought," said Doctor Cohen, dropping the bottles into his bag and snapping the clasp. "She must have been taking less than she said. Ah well, in charge to the last. Good day to you both."

"Yes, indeed. Thank you so much for coming so quickly." She wanted him to know that he had done his job as well as he could. Perhaps she should tell him, reassure him she knew the job well enough, that her father would have done it just the same, but she could not find the will within her to be so intimate and extend the conversation.

"I will show you out, Doctor," said Oliver.

"Most kind."

Oliver escorted him down the hall and out. He walked back into the room and sat down. He took Beatrix's hand.

"And so, it begins. My God, I am sorry. I know this bit only too well. A man who was very dear to me died suddenly and with no reason. I found him, very much as you found Dora, dead in bed. I had come to collect him, we were off to see *Oh, Julie* at the Shaftesbury of all things that evening. He must have taken an afternoon nap and never woke up . . ."

"How old were you?"

"Twenty-four."

"Very young . . ."

Oliver shrugged. ". . .To be in a relationship with an older man? Not sure you of all people can claim that. How old were you when you met Dora?"

"You are right and this will shock you – I was nineteen and she was twenty-nine!"

"Fresh off the milk train from Durham?"

"Just about . . . well, I was green, at any roads. Dora seemed to be so sophisticated to my eyes – she knew Vera from their finishing school in Switzerland. Dora's parents scraped together the money, but didn't have enough to finish off her sister Matilde when the time came, which was the cause of much of the subsequent difficulty between them."

"I had no idea Dora came from such a highflying family – a deb no less."

"I wouldn't go that far. It all came from her father's side, and they only managed to cover the sum required for the first six months. She always joked that she wasn't finished enough. Sorry, this is classic grief talk, isn't it? Burbling on in small circles."

"Important and fascinating, please don't worry. Keep going, tell me about when you met."

"At a suffrage gathering – a tea party. I'd been invited by a girl at work and Vera and Mary brought Dora. Vera always fancied herself as having a brain, though I saw little evidence of it over the years. It wasn't love at first sight by any means, it took us a couple of years of friendship before we allowed ourselves to be closer. Though Dora was older, she was in fact the younger in terms of reconciling herself to her attraction to women. I often wonder; if we had never met, I am fairly sure she would have married . . . unhappily for her, but very much wanted by her mother. Our families had no idea. Even our sisters, as far as we could tell, were purposefully blind, but then again, we did nothing to enlighten them."

"And in my case necessary."

"Frankly, it might as well be illegal for us the way we have to deal with it. The social disapproval is almost as effective as the law. So, you found that poor man dead you say."

"Yes, and like you I knew, and I could not believe it, all at the same time. My lover was a friend of Vera and Mary's – that's how I found my way to the Gateways."

"My goodness, those two were the glue that held us all together. Never made a song and dance about it though, did they?"

"Nurses often don't. Just get on with the show."

The thought of that kind of attitude pulled Beatrix back to the present. "Why didn't Dora say about the Angina? That is what is so hard now that she's gone. I can't ask her . . . or more truthfully . . . shout at her."

"Sudden death however it happens, is far worse for those left behind they say, and I think they are right. Easier on the dead but tougher on the living. My chap's family tipped up almost immediately and took over. It was as if I had never existed. Even as a so called 'dear friend' I had no say, though some others did. Because I was younger than him it made it easier, or perhaps imperative, for them to kick over the traces of our life together. I went to the funeral, though I dreaded it. It was a ceremony for a man that never existed."

"Well, I will definitely make sure I am in charge of the funeral come what may."

"Oh, Beatrix I am so sorry you must face this along with everything else. The next of kin bit just now with Doctor Cohen was so painful."

"Don't worry about me, I have been too long in the game to be thrown by the inevitable difficulties caused by our pathetic subterfuges. Choices were made. There is, in fact, a niece somewhere, the daughter of the long-dead Matilde, but I wasn't going to say that to Doctor Cohen. Dora's attitude was, at best, ambivalent to her. There is, in fact, a will. I know where it is . . . upstairs in my bedside table drawer. I told Dora there was little point, the house and shop are in my name, we agreed that was simplest as I was most likely to survive her. As you know, our circumstances are such that there won't be anything to leave."

"Did the niece know Dora well? Do you know her?"

"No, we never met. After Matilde died there was very little contact. Dora had the feeling the niece cared little for her and as I said the sisters were never close, particularly once Matilde moved to France. I suppose, now I think of it, that was something in life we shared."

Oliver checked his watch. "Beatrix, I don't quite know how to say this – but I must go. I need to catch the train into town, though I really don't want to have to leave you."

"Of course you do, you must. I would not have it otherwise, indeed Dora wouldn't. This day was always going to come. I will cope, I always do."

"What will you do?"

"Phone Underhill's and get them round. Sort a few things. Put the hens to bed. The usual."

"That's the ticket. Routine. No dashing off to Durham?"

"Exactly."

"I will come back tomorrow morning first thing and be with you when the dreaded Miss Moyle comes. You can't face that on your own and we must think about next steps. The bailiffs will have to be called off whilst you sort things out here and make arrangements for the funeral and all that follows."

"Go and meet your agent. Please don't worry about me. I will call the bank first thing and tell them. The bailiffs will, I am sure, be called off to give me time to put my affairs in order."

"No, I am not having it. I will return in the morning. First thing. Find out how you are."

"Go now, or you will be late. I have kept you far too long."

"Not before I see you stand up and walk about the room."

Beatrix rose to her feet. The adrenaline of dealing with the doctor and the certainty of Dora's death had steadied her legs and cleared her head. "Look, I am fine. Breathing steady, head clear. I will go into the garden, get some air . . . just as soon as you are gone."

"Will you be able to cope alone with Underhill's this evening?"

"Yes, don't worry, I will be fine. Doctor Cohen says they are a very good firm. They will look after me just as much as Dora, I suspect. You go — and despite all this for goodness' sake enjoy yourself."

She walked with him down the hall to the front door. The sun was striking the front of the house in a blaze, the amber light of an autumnal late afternoon giving its final burnishing, before sinking behind the houses opposite.

"What a sight," he said, unable to stop himself from

being happy at his good fortune. She could tell from his expression that he was checking himself, selfish that he had allowed his pleasure to show.

"Yes, lovely." She wanted him to know she didn't mind, that in truth she would be glad to be on her own. She folded her arms and leaned on the doorpost, feeling the warmth of the sun on her, within her.

"You mustn't worry about me. I suppose it's easier for those who have a faith like you and in her way Dora, but Dora never feared death and neither do I. When the time comes it comes. We have both had a wonderful life, we always said that to each other. Whatever terrible things have happened in the world ... and goodness knows there have been many terrible things in our time ... we know we have lived a good life and been responsible for none of its shortcomings. Thank you so much for staying, for being here. You were just perfect in everything you did and the way that you did it. You must forget this now and go on with your own affairs. 'Where there is life there is hope' as they say ..."

"Not so easy, Miss Veal. I will return tomorrow. When you posted that letter this morning you wanted me to come, but my role is not to be as you thought it ..."

"I hope you understand it was because of our friendship and because of the person you are. I hope you are flattered, and I hope I am forgiven."

"I have taken it as the compliment I know you meant it to be."

"It was. It is." She looked at him standing there so smart, so much to look forward to. "Will you go to the King's Head to celebrate?"

"I just might."

"Give my love to Carlyle Square if you pass through.

Dora and I used to head there to talk and canoodle after the Gateways chucked us out at the end of an evening – or should I say at the beginning of the morning – and we tottered down the road. I recall us being found there one night by a couple of older club members and we were well and truly OUT as a couple."

"I will make a point of doing so, for Dora. I am most dreadfully sorry about the immensity of your loss. I know just how much Dora means to you," he said, kissing her on the cheek, something she realised he had never done before. He put his hat on to his head and headed off down the road to the bus and the London train.

Beatrix lingered on the doorstep. The touch of the sun felt good on her skin – soothing. The stove should be getting up-to-speed now. She would feed it and it would help to warm the rest of the house. She should leave the bedroom fire off though; not wise to heat the room. She was relieved she was alone. The house felt resigned after the turmoil of the last hours, though everything about the place had changed. Behind her back nothing was as it had been, in front of her the world carried on just the same, regardless. It was as if she had dived under the water's surface and was swimming, eyes open, looking back at the shoreline from a world submerged – transformed. She might have a bath; float away the backache that Doctor Cohen warned her of. The thought of lying in warm water, suspended, felt highly attractive – though she very much doubted that she had the energy for all that drawing, carrying, and pouring.

As she thought to go in, Fred arrived on his bike to empty the post box of its afternoon letters.

"Lovely evening, isn't it?" he called to her, "after all that mist this morning."

"Lovely."

"Nothing in my delivery bag this afternoon for you, or Miss Ham, I am afraid."

"Well, that is a relief."

"I suppose so. Good day to you, Miss Veal."

"Good day." She had a moment's hesitation when she might have called him back – might have asked him if there was something he had in his possession to deliver for Mr Cope tomorrow morning by any chance – but, lost as to what she would say next, she closed the front door.

She went straight to the scullery and checked the stove, as she had done at least ten times each day. The empty coal scuttle caught her attention. She was relieved to feel herself getting back into her usual stride. What was Dora's contribution to the daily routine? Breakfast, that was all.

She put on her coat and hen hat, grabbed the pan of yesterday's scraps along with the empty scuttle and headed out to the garden. She dropped the scuttle by the bunker and walked down the garden path. She threw the scraps over the chicken wire fence to the murmuring crowd; devoured in an instant. A rust-encrusted shovel was lying in the shadows of the bunker, she pushed it into the pile of coals and the bitter-smelling black soot; one, two, three, four, five shovels full did the trick. As she straightened her stiff back, she noticed the garden was in shadow and considerably cooler than at the front. She looked back at the hens, they were still scratching about for any remaining morsels – ever hopeful; she had better usher them in, the sun was sinking at a rapid pace.

She walked past the hens to the fence at the bottom of the garden. The horse was nowhere to be seen. Probably wandered closer to the gate at the side, or he may have been taken in by now as the days were drawing short and the nights long. The hens were beginning to shuffle up the gang planks of their own accord – the chill in the air increasing their levels of anxiety and motivating them inside. She wouldn't bother to collect any of today's laying – they could spend the night warmed by a feathery bottom for other hands to hold tomorrow. Was it wrong of those other women to join the choir of voices that encouraged hands to turn eggs into missiles all those years ago? *A wanton waste of a good meal* her father called it, though he had no idea Dora and Beatrix were involved in peacefully campaigning for the vote.

Wondering if a hen found an egg comforting or uncomfortable, she shut the two side doors – the movement of which caused a panic in the remaining stragglers as they ran for the hen house, pushing and flapping their way in, the weaker falling by the wayside and having to run round to the bottom of the plank and start again.

"You really are the stupidest of creatures – take your time ladies, take your time."

What you see in those birds I will never know, dear.

"Scrambled eggs and roast chicken mostly, Dora. Also, a little of you if I am honest about it."

Don't be then.

The hens all-in, she slid the big door shut, let herself out of their enclosure and began to walk the chicken wire boundary line, pressing in a turf here, bending back a wire there. It looked secure enough to last the night out from the foxes' attention. As she came round to the far side, the last of the sun's light was hitting the very part of the copse where she and Oliver had stood earlier, looking back at this garden, foolish and unaware of what was going on inside as Dora quietly slipped off the stage. How extraordinary that she had suggested they walk there – one of her last requests as she unwittingly went up the stairs. Thinking of everything and knowing nothing. When had been the last time that Dora had gone for a walk? God only knows.

The copse was floating again on the brow of the hill – the effect this evening caused by the tips of the trees glowing in the last of the rays, turning them back into the role of metaphor; though beautiful the Elysian Fields must have been a jolly boring place. Why had she thought so much this morning about limbo when she was out here – indeed where was Dora now? Her body was in the bedroom but where was she? Could she see Beatrix standing in her garden looking up? Waving would be silly, yet Dora felt so close, just there, and here and all around. It was an infectiously comforting feeling that Dora was still with her: in the air, in the breeze, in the amber light, the essence of Dora in the essence of everything. Spilt into a million, billion atoms and yet still sentient – still thinking – still observing – still speaking through memory. She reached out and held the thin air in her cupped hands. Did she truly want to feel that Dora was watching her every move? Was that comforting or terrifying? She hoped she would come to find she could turn this feeling of Dora's presence on and off at will.

"Are you there Dora?" she spoke into her cupped hands. "Come on now, a sign ... you damn well promised me a sign."

She stood. Listening hard, feeling the breeze move across her face. She closed her eyes. She stretched out her long arms in a crucifix and leaned forward, inviting anything and everything to reveal itself to her. A rook cawed. A dog barked. Not very original, Dora. The hens shuffled in their boxes – definitely not that. The backdrop of traffic hummed on the arterial road. Perhaps it would work if she was with Dora upstairs, it would be easier somehow – although if it was to be anywhere it would be here, it would be now, surely. She waited. Nothing.

She opened her eyes and resumed walking the chicken wire boundary line round to the gate at the start, all was shipshape. She turned and was heading up the path, back up to the house to face whatever was next, when a large hare – perhaps tempted in by the hope of some rotten vegetables and then taken cover when she came out of the house – pelted past her. Its one sideways brown eye stared right at her, holding hers with a firm gaze as it ran. Long legs at full stretch, it shot through the bars of the fence to the field beyond and it was gone. She had never seen a live hare – always hoped but never seen. Its image was imprinted in her mind's eye, such had been the strength of the hare's presence. To be that close to such a wild thing was a gift. Maybe it was a sign? She stared at the place it had come from – retracing the route; she wished it back – she wished she could move time back two minutes and have it all again, the moment was too fleeting. She stood stock-still hoping the hare would come again. Yet she knew it was not Dora.

Chapter Eight

Back in the house the pantry was warm. The hungry stove took nearly the whole scuttle-full. She shut and locked the back door and hung up her hen coat and hat. She stood in the kitchen – what now? She put the kettle on. Yes, that was what you did. The phone rang. She was afraid Doctor Cohen might have contacted Underhill's himself. Afterall, he had noticed her reticence at doing anything. She could hardly just let it ring – it might be something important. She went to the hall table; twenty-one, twenty-two, twenty – whoever this was they meant it.

"Hello?"

"Beatrix, it's me … it's Alice."

"Oh Alice. I am sorry, I …" she let her words trail off. Poor Alice, quite forgotten.

"I tried to call you twice."

"Yes, yes, I know. I am sorry, Alice … I …" what was she to say?

"Harold and I have had a chat, and we feel, under the circumstances, that we have little option but to offer you a roof. For a time. Whilst you sort out what to do. Certainly, only for a short time – for Dora. We had considered not welcoming Dora, but we cannot find it in our hearts to be that cruel, the circumstances such as they are."

This had taken a lot of rehearsing with Harold. Even if the delivery was staccato, it was kind, far kinder than she had expected. As soon as she heard Alice's voice, she knew she was not going to tell her about Dora; she must stick to that line. Otherwise, Alice might surprisingly jump on a train and arrive, shattering her privacy. She needed time to work out the next steps, put things in order before the bailiff's inevitable return visit. Silence about Dora created a bubble of protection; no one knew, but Oliver and the doctor – better kept that way, better things kept simple. She couldn't face the questions she didn't have an answer to. Play for a bit of time.

"Alice, that's kind of you. Really very, very kind when it was such an ask and so out of the blue. Truly grateful ... but ... something has come up that changes things and I need a moment to take it in and work out what to do. So, we have a bit of time, days perhaps, which will be a relief to you both I'm sure – as much as me. Let's leave things for a day or so and then arrangements can be made when things are more sorted here."

"How so? That you have time?"

All the best lies have some degree of truth about them. Beatrix tried her best to knit two worlds together. "A friend, a dear friend arrived today ... out of the blue ... and having discovered our circumstances ... wants to see if he can put the bailiffs off for a while, delay things a bit so we can make a proper plan. It's worth a try, a conversation with the bank to just see ... it will probably come to nothing ... but it's worth a try."

"Well, are you sure? Taking a bit of time does sound more sensible. Calm even."

"Oh yes, it is all very calm here now."

"If, you are sure? It's very kind of this friend – are you sure?"

"Taking time now is sensible . . . as you say. Something came up that has slowed everything down. It's very kind of you both – after all – I haven't been in touch that much, have I?"

"Well . . . that fault probably rests with us both."

The silence yo-yoed down the line between them. For all her need of being alone, Beatrix found it hard to end the call.

"Alice? When was the last time you were in Scarborough?"

"Talk about out of the blue questions! Oh, now let me think – I honestly can't recall – not for absolutely ages and ages. Why?"

"I was remembering it today and wondering if they still have the donkeys."

"I'm sure they do – what would Scarborough beach be without the donkeys? My goodness Beattie, how you loved those smelly old things. Daddy and I never understood it."

"Eyes open; mouth closed?"

"Sorry?"

"Eyes open; mouth closed – what he used to say to me trying to teach me to swim on that beach – and I determinedly kept my eyes shut and my mouth wide open."

"You were a terrible swimmer – you always were."

"Well, I got my watch for doing twenty strokes – still wear it every day."

"Of course you do. I have no idea where mine went. You should go. When you come – you should go to Scarborough – see if the donkeys are still there. I might even join you."

"Maybe . . ." She needed to end this now it was becoming unbearable, overly polite and heartbreaking. "Maybe . . . maybe sometime. Thanks, thanks for the call. Goodbye Alice," said Beatrix, as she put the receiver down.

In her day she had tried to be a good older sister. When had it come – that separation? Their childhood was close enough in years for them to always be *my little ducks*, as their father called them; slow, quiet Sundays, creeping round the house not disturbing him, snoozing after lunch on the one day off from his patients. In their Sunday School pinafores, in their white mutton-sleeve blouses. How old? When does memory start? Snatches of her mother – wisps of emotion more than memory; so faint, she was almost sure they were invented. Kneeling next to her mother, the knee covered by her long skirt but present against Beatrix's resting spine and the tug of her mother brushing her hair; at the beach, sitting high up on a donkey looking down at her mother's freckled face from on high, her mother's arm round Beatrix's toddler-straight back – her mother's auburn hair loosening out of her bun – laughing. These were memories denied for poor little Alice. Why did no one talk about it? Out of sight out of mind – what a fiasco, but Beatrix had seen the heaviness of the bent shape of the winding sheet as they took the body down the stairs, as Alice's newborn lungs mewled from the centre of her parent's bed, the birthing and the death room combined in one moment in time. She supposed he was consumed by guilt – being the cause of his wife's death on two counts – the impregnator and the professional failure who could not save her. No one could make that pain go away; no man could admit that to his daughters. He never spoke about it and, in time, she learned to follow his example in emotional self-protection methods. No wonder Beatrix's inability to reveal her heart's innermost feelings – handed down like the family silver – drove Dora to distraction.

How had it been then as they grew up? She should try to work it out. She remembered sitting with Alice and cutting her fringe. *Let me do it, it will be fine ... sit still Alice.* The wise older sister who would sort these things now their mother was gone. But it wasn't fine at all, no matter how much she tried, and Alice had cried and been so cross and unforgiving, milking the moment for Daddy. It took months to grow back, with gentle regular shaping from Mrs Goswell next door and Beatrix allowed nowhere near it. Maybe that was it – she ruined things for Alice by existing – splitting the reduced parental affection reduced its value. Just by being, Beatrix was a threat. After she left the two of them alone and went to London, she felt that at last Alice had things as she wished them – sole control over her Daddy. Something was lost that day for Beatrix and her father. Never spoken but a gentle coolness grew between them and once allowed to grow, over time it strengthened to a silence; warm-hearted Alice stayed, and hard-hearted Beatrix left. She never told either of them about what Dora was to her, the special love that was found, the companion-ship, the coming of age; Beatrix had decided from the start it was better that way and that was how it had remained, official companions. Then Daddy's funeral, organised by Alice and attended by Beatrix, threw enough cold water on the embers of their remaining affection that the years passed by *going through the motions*, as Dora would say.

Beatrix wiped her hand over the veneer on the telephone table and rubbed any possible dust that might have gathered since her last visit into the palms of her hand. She could not motivate her fingers to dial the number for Underhill's. She stood up and adjusted the chair, so it was straight on to the table and wiped her hand along the back of it – it made her think of the bent spine of a skeleton. What should the order of things be? She checked her watch. It was nearly five o'clock. Oliver would return in the morning, she knew that, and then Miss Moyle. Probably the bank would be unable to stop the bailiffs however early they were called, but now she had all the time in the world. It was about three hours since she came home and found Dora, yet it felt like a lifetime.

She passed through to the scullery and into the shop to give it the once over, switching on the overhead light as she passed by. She rarely allowed herself to eat the sweets, much to Dora's infuriation. She walked down the row and pulled down a jar of sherbet lemons. She opened the screw top jar and took out a bullet-shaped lozenge.

I say, Alice, what have you got there?

Sherbet lemon.

What are you doing silly? You will drop it in the sand holding it that way, let me show you. You must crinkle it back and forth between your first finger and thumb, in just a couple of rubs, otherwise it makes a disgusting sticky mess like you have made of this one.

I haven't got another.

Yes, you have, in the pocket of your pinafore dress – come on then, hand it over. See, like this Alice. Two rubs and it's out. If you work at it with you tongue you get a hole at the end and you can suck all the sherbet out.

Beatrix crinkled the yellow cellophane between her finger and thumb, releasing the sweet like a seed from a pod and popped it in her mouth. *Enough sugar in the shop to kill the whole of Durham.* Their father had a mortal fear of the stuff – knowing too much, although it turned out too little, about the deadly sickness of diabetes. He felt the cause to be sugar, not the failure of the body, but the overdose of the sweet. His distant disapproval keenly felt, pushing its way south down the train track, shamed that his daughter ran, of all things, a sweetshop; had he lived long enough to see it he would have been a great supporter of war rationing continuing forever. Though she lived off the proceeds of selling sugar, personal denial of the pleasure of sweet treats had been part of Beatrix's life, which she now came to think of as being out of a sense of duty – first imposed, then embraced. The sourness of the sherbet felt good. Cleansing.

Despite the disapproval, their first years were not that bad. There was a business and there was a garden to grow. They fixed the house, they made the shop, they stayed screwed tight and in their shell, two co-habiting hermit crabs – not entirely at home but close enough to fitting in. And then Oliver came, and it felt hopeful, for her if not for Dora. Why had she resented him so? Dora's world had turned so inward. Was she agoraphobic? Beatrix had never considered this before. Certainly, the great outdoors increasingly held no charm for Dora; even the things she enjoyed, like trips to London, became out of bounds. Beatrix had thought this was because her legs had given up on her and that certainly was Dora's excuse. Yet perhaps it was her heart that had given up – both physically and emotionally. Dora's world became the shop and the house – not even the garden was visited. And so, for Beatrix, Oliver became freedom – the garden and her commitments to Oliver the only escape.

You might as well leave me for him – a mariage blanc would suit you both down to the ground.

Beatrix dumped the jar of sherbet lemons down on the counter. It was time to fight back.

"You were the one being ridiculous Dora – surely you

didn't begrudge me a walk once a week – it's not as if I went into town with him to wild parties."

You could have done; it was all the same to me.

"But you were the dancer – the party girl. Where did she go Dora?"

My legs were too tired, I would rather have done nothing than do something badly . . . and besides, dancing in old age was not a look I wanted to perfect – everyone staring at the stupid old bag.

"Why didn't you ever say about your heart? It was cruel of you never to tell me . . ."

. . . and besides who should I have as a partner . . .?

"Oh, low blow, low blow . . . now that you are dead you really do feel obliged to put the boot in don't you dear . . ."

Gracious in defeat is the best way to face old age, as you will come to discover for yourself.

"Gracious in defeat is not a phrase that comes easily to mind when I think of you Dora."

Don't then . . .

And Beatrix hurled the jar of sherbet lemons right across the room, smashing the bell off its rocker and exploding against the door frame. Boiled sweets and glass shards cascaded onto the floor and the bell bounced across the shop. She threw her head back and laughed in a way she had not felt free to do in years.

"Oh Dora, Dora how I damn well miss you . . ." she shouted to the empty shop.

She stood staring at the wreckage. Why had she come in here in the first place? The Barnardo's boy stood hopefully in the corner, but there was nothing for his charity box – Dora had already seen to right that wrong with her donation from the till earlier in the day, in as much as she could. Beatrix ran her fingers down the row of books on the shelf behind her counter, the catalogue of all the ins and outs of the business. Separate accounts for the sweet-shop and post office. The story, if anyone cared to look, of how it all went slowly, oh so slowly, downhill. All done in Beatrix's neat spider handwriting. She unlocked the drawer that no longer had any need to be locked since she was removed from her duties. She had loved the rules and the regulations: the times to be open and the times to be closed. Sometimes this caused confusion – sweet shop open and post office closed – it kept the customers guessing. She put away the stamps, the wet sponge, her cash tin. She placed her hand on the small brass weighing machine. She watched the spindle move up the ounces as she pressed the small platform on which she would place the letters. Each grade had a price. 2½d for up to 2oz, 3d for up to 4oz, 4d for up to 6oz. The tall white parcel weighing machine had been requisitioned; she had made sure she was out when that day came.

It had been a slow stripping, now she thought about it. From the letting go of her London self, the Gateways, the theatre, the gin and bridge parties at Vera and Mary's, the coffees at Dickins & Jones. Then the new suburban persona. As a sub-postmistress she grew an even harder shell, became a more private person, had a more private life with Dora – no place to let herself go. Then the biggest, nastiest strip of all: her dignity, her pride, her ability to defend them both from the reality of the dream life Dora had chosen – no, as she had previously acknowledged that wasn't fair, it was a life they had both persuaded themselves to believe in. Now she could, she let her hatred of the dreariness of village life flow though her. Ghastly people, small minds, small lives.

You are such a snob, dear.

"No, Dora – a realist. They were ghastly and Terry the

ghastliest of all the ghastlies. That damn man. He blighted our lives and, no doubt, the lives to come of so many others, upping the rent till he squeezes them out."

What would it have cost him to let them be? In the end he would get the house, the shop and all that went with it, and he knew it would not have been long. He could have let them see out their days – with perhaps a little help from Alice – but she didn't want to think about that – no, not that call – *Are you asking me for money Beatrix after all this time?*

Oh no, not that. But little people like Terry didn't have an imagination, a soul. Ambitious little shit of a man – a classic bully who never, ever, ever, had to accommodate another person's dreams in their lives. No, Terry would be looked after to the end of his days by that sad little mousey woman who crept about the village in her pleated skirt, with her wicker shopping basket full of shop-bought eggs.

Eggs. Now there's a thought.

She found one of Miss Moyle's much-adored pretty cards of this morning. She took the cap off her fountain pen and began to write slowly and carefully.

Dear Muriel,

I trust this note finds you well enough. I am so sorry about the mix up with the newspaper this morning. I hope you found the Manchester Guardian of interest. I can highly recommend taking a separate paper from your husband. It will broaden your mind – though I suspect that's not something Terry will want to encourage.

I do hope you are happy with your life. If not, I beg you to consider an alternative to the world view according to Tit-Bits. We all have choices. The question is, are we brave enough to take them?

I am not ashamed of what I have done today. Bullies need to be called out.
Yours,
Beatrix Veal

She licked the envelope and wrote:
Private Addressee Only – *Mrs Muriel Longhurst*
This felt so good.

She turned round and swept a large cache of account books into her arms. Why should she follow the rules and keep them for all to see? She took them through to the scullery, opened the stove door and threw them into the hot coals, making three trips before it was all done. Quite an alarming amount of flame and smoke was coming from the stove, but she shut the door and let them be. She went back into the shop and grabbed the envelope off the counter before returning to the scullery to find a large bowl. She checked the stove – it was calmer. She put the eggs, one, two, eight, eleven, fifteen ... into the bowl, covering it with a cloth, and put on her town coat and town hat, secured with a hat pin.

Not sure I approve of this ... but a nice touch, dear.

She placed the envelope in her pocket, grabbed the bowl and her keys and left the house through the front door, locking it behind her. The sun was dropping down fast behind the houses; it would be dark soon. She turned right and hurried though the village. Terry's house was on the other side of the green. She crossed the road, taking the short route over the grass to the pond. The white ducks were silent, gliding, keeping their heads down. She supposed they had to stay out there in the middle all night for fear of the foxes, poor things, no one to care. As she was crossing the road on the far side of the green, she heard a screech of bicycle brakes.

"Good evening, Miss Veal!"

Turning, she saw it was William. "Ah, William, of course," she said, feeling dangerously light-headed and almost openly giggling. "How funny to see you."

"In what way?"

"I mean typical, not funny. Typical that I should bump into you." The boy looked at her with his head on one side.

"Just out on an errand, must get on ..." it was time to get away before she said anything silly.

"Sure. Shall I come tonight?"

"No, really, don't bother – there isn't a job that needs doing." Honesty was the best policy now.

"OK, well, I guess I'll see you in the morning then." And he made to stand on his pedals.

"Ah no, William, you won't. I'm afraid the shop is now shut until further notice. It has been a sudden thing for all of us, but there we are. I am sorry to let you down in this way."

"So, you mean you don't need me anymore?" The boy looked utterly crestfallen.

"No, I am sorry. I should have said before, but no, we don't need you anymore. It's not our decision I'm afraid. Larger elements at play." She looked down the road to Terry's house. "Specifically, Mr Longhurst. If you want to ask why, ask him. I would be grateful if you would tell your mother. In fact, ask her to ask him, will you? Good afternoon." And she sped on down the road before she had to look at his face another minute. Another victim. Another victim of Terry Longhurst had bitten the dust.

The lights were off in the house. Where was Muriel? Creeping about in the gloom to save money no doubt. She went up the path, tapped the envelope twice on the back of her hand and pushed the note to Muriel though the letterbox. Terry's beloved silver Singer car was, as she had hoped, reversed into the short drive; its nose touched the pavement end of the driveway, perfectly lit, like a prized statue, by the streetlamp. For maximum pleasure she needed to do this from a reasonable distance. Stepping back onto the road she looked up and down – empty – before peeling back the cloth, and slap, the first egg hit the windscreen. She could hear the voices from the crowd behind her, the tune playing out in her head, and she began to sing something she hadn't sung for years; like the Lord's prayer the words just fell into place.

> Life, strife, these two are one,
> Nought can ye win but by faith and daring:
> On, on that ye have done,
> But for the work of today preparing.
> Firm in reliance, laugh a defiance,
> (Laugh in hope, for sure is the end)
> March, march, many as one.
> Shoulder to Shoulder and friend to friend.

Slap, slap, slap. On and on it went, the bowl not yet empty, smash, smash, smash. She checked the road again. She stepped further back for the final onslaught, which she threw with all her might. The whole screen was a delicious yellowish smear flecked with broken shells. She picked up the bowl and smacked it down with all the force within her on the bonnet. She didn't care if Muriel came out. It left a very satisfying dent. She picked up the bowl from where it had fallen and crashed it down again, and again and again until it shattered.

Silence. She wiped her brow and settled her hat with its

pin. The sounds of the village returned to her. A ginger cat picked its way past, a swishing tail the only part of its body to reveal any concern caused by the changed world that surrounded it. As her blind-rage drained, a terror crept over her and finding her basket at her feet she grabbed it and fled back over the green and down the road to the shop. Her trembling hands struggled to find the keys in her pocket; she must unlock the door, she could sense someone behind her – surely. She fell though the doorway, slammed the door, locked it and leaned back, breathing as if her lungs could not suck in the air fast enough. Her legs were shaking. She dropped her basket and wiped the sweat from her face with her coat before flinging it and her hat to the hall floor.

"I'm back. I did it! I did it, Dora!" she called wildly up the stairs, to the dead silence above.

Chapter Nine

Her head felt clear. What a circle the day had been. From waking with Dora and believing it was their last day, then to feeling that somehow life could go on, to Dora dying, to smashing eggs, to now.

Forcing her legs to hold her, she climbed the stairs but stopped with her hand on the bedroom door handle. As sure as she had ever been about anything, she knew that Dora's soul would be released when she opened the door. It was time. She turned the handle and as she pushed the door open there was a sucking, like an inward breath, followed by the coolest breeze of air that gently kissed her hand, went up her arm, then her neck and brushed her cheek. It moved upwards though her hair, she could feel it on her scalp, it lifted from her and passed onwards. As she turned, following its flow, it evaporated into the air above the banisters. No more chatting; Dora had departed. Beatrix was alone. Now, at this moment of parting, her mind became fixed, it was her task to follow – but how? She looked down into the stairwell and held on to the banister. The drop was enough. She felt the banister – it appeared strong, but did she have the guts? Doctor Cohen had removed all the sleeping pills; the gas was all out in the meter and though she could refill it, that amount of gas in a draughty bedroom would never be enough to complete the job. There was a dressing gown cord in the back bedroom, she would look for it in a while. Staring down she began to feel dizzy again, for goodness's sake. She breathed in and out slowly, no rush, no rush – only when the time felt right.

She opened the door and was shocked to find the room and Dora's body not quite as she had left it. Presumably Doctor Cohen, she doubted Oliver, had switched on the bedside light on Dora's side of the bed and drawn the curtains. Worse, he had moved her into a formal pose by turning her so that she lay straight legged on her back, mouth and eyes shut. The eiderdown and blanket were set aside – folded on the chair. The white sheet stretched tight across Dora's body and tucked with hospital corners. At the top end the sheet was neatly turned down under Dora's arms, her hands crossed and resting on her stomach, like a knight on top of a tomb in Durham Cathedral. The discarded shell of Dora looked both at rest and supremely uncomfortable at the same time. Formal, an acceptable death pose, she supposed. The unmade-up face looked stern and unsettled, so she set to work with Dora's makeup bag from the dressing table to make amends. She checked the chin and upper lip for straggly hairs with the small gold-backed magnifying glass that Dora had used for checking her own. Neither of them could bear to become the hairy old ladies they derided so much in their youth; Dora often spoke darkly about her Aunt Agatha in this vein, whist chasing her own foibles round with the twee-zers. Some blue eye shadow to the lids, a bit of rouge to the cheeks – far less than Dora would use – a slick of lipstick to the obliging lips, a dab of the Eau de Cologne, a puff of powder to forehead, cheeks, and chin. She considered the elements of Dora's jewellery that she was still wearing. The brooch could go back onto the neck of her blouse; the signet ring back onto her little finger, the rest would make her look ridiculously over dressed – even for Dora. Leaning back, she admired her work – she hoped she had achieved a look in which Dora would be prepared to meet her undertaker. If only she had been allowed to do this more towards the end, she might have protected Dora from being an object of derision by those girls in the shop. Glasses on or off she wondered. She let them lie on the bedside table, enough was enough.

Dora had talked earlier about taking the theatre programme collection to Durham. Beatrix had not reminded her for fear of time slipping whilst Dora relived her days, but they were in a trunk and under the bed. She bent down and peered into the dusty gloom. More dead skin she supposed. She reached in and felt around until her hand found the bony ribs of the carcass breaking through the stretched leather. She fumbled along to the leather strap handle and pulled with all her might. They had both struggled to push it under here – how many years ago? Certainly, they had not had this out for a long time. How on earth it could have made its way, or fitted in at Alice's would have been anybody's guess. No need for that now.

Slowly the trunk shifted and slid out from under the bed. She dragged it into the middle of the bedroom and having wiped away the worst of the dust with Dora's hanky she clicked the two rusty metal clasps and lifted the lid, which yawned wide on its metal straps. The overpowering smell of mildew was the first thing to hit her as she gazed down on year upon year of theatre trips. She knew that at the very bottom would be Dora's childhood visits with her mother, father and Matilde, up on the bus from Balham.

The surface layer was the glossy, if mottled, records of their final trips. She picked up one. *Black Velvet* at the London Hippodrome. She could remember them standing at the stage door, Dora shifting from foot to foot, wishing them to be allowed in. There were always long periods of suspense after the request was made and the fear of rejection from Dora palpable. Beatrix looked at the blue/black and white photographs of the pretty young faces staring back at her, their slick hair curled and coiffed, their eyebrows thin pencil lines, their full lips inviting, some leaning back in a state of bliss, clutching a chiffon scarf. Several holding a cigarette in a manicured hand. The chorus were a line of unremembered faces lost in time. But the starlet shots were all helpfully named: Iris Lockwood, Pat Kirkbride, Mary Evans – where were they now?

Here was another – *Operette* by Noël Coward. Dora must have gone to this one with someone else as Beatrix had no recollection. In each of the programmes nestled the tickets, and sometimes the order for the tea, if it was a matinee. Dora was incredibly partial to a matinee tea – served by stern ladies in black bombazine, white aprons, and little white caps. The trays with unfolding legs were passed down the rows, your neighbours entirely in charge of how much tea or milk was slopped over your triangles of sandwiches and a small fancy cake. Beatrix found it a fuss about nothing in terms of the quality – the tea stewed and cool, the miserable sandwiches curly – but the performance of it amused her. It was often the case, particularly at The Hippodrome, that the show was vacuous and overly frothy for her taste, so watching the progress of the laden and then the empty trays passing back and forth was often the best part of the afternoon.

She shifted the heavy piles around trying to find *Peter Pan* and what was the other that Dora had mentioned? *Journey's End*? Buried deep in the sediment of hundreds of hours of forgotten spills and thrills, or dreadful let downs. Dora kept them all, whether she enjoyed the show or not. She tried once more to find them, but it was impossible without tipping the whole lot out and spending an age sifting through the piles. Why was she looking anyway – it didn't matter. She could hardly have them be found with her clutching the programme of *Peter Pan* and Dora *Journey's End*. She slid the programmes back into place and closed the trunk. It could stay where it rested.

Moving over to the other side of the bed she realised she had been distracted from her purpose in coming up here in the first place – she needed to find the wills. They had nominated this drawer in the bedside table on 'her' side for their wills to be kept; everyone immediately goes for the bedside cabinets when searching for clues. They were written many years ago, after a bruising session, having received a letter from Vera that painfully detailed her terrible experience of being totally cut out of everything after the unexpected death of Mary. They had not bothered with a lawyer – these little notes had been simple enough to write, though on reflection, after that chat with Doctor Cohen earlier, that decision had probably been unwise. They left everything to the other and agreed the living could make the decision about what to do after that, no hands tied. When the plan had been to go together, they decided to change nothing. The tautologous circle seemed fitting – for nothing will come of nothing; Terry Longhurst could have all he wanted, and Dora said Matilde's daughter Celeste wanted for nothing. In turn Beatrix had said nothing in her will about Alice, but what could she have bequeathed that had any meaning?

The two thin envelopes were there in the drawer, marked rather tartly after some discussion, '*To Whom It May Concern*'; it felt like the best clue to the contents. She sat on her side of the bed and pulled the envelopes out. A little dropper-bottle, no more than two inches high, rolled forward from the back of the drawer. Long forgotten, Doctor Cohen's laudanum tincture, prescribed when her back was so bad she could not get out of bed for a week. How long ago? At least ten years – and yet he had not forgotten about it when he asked her. Was he remembering the laudanum, then, wondering if she still had it? He was no fool, he had taken the sleeping pills.

He above all people knew what grief could do.

She switched on the bedside light on her side and held it up to the lamp. The bottle was brown and the liquid dark, so it was hard to see how much was there. It looked possible that the dropper was immersed up to its shoulders. 'Laudanum. Poppy Opium. Take with caution.' it said, in large print in Doctor Cohen's neat handwriting. 'Dosage: one drop in a tumbler of water, to a maximum of two drops per day, for no more than three days at a time.'

She recalled her dread of taking it when it was prescribed it for her. Her father always carried a small bottle in his bag but was careful to put it away in a high cupboard on returning home after his rounds. As the eldest he had taken to confiding in her about his patients. He told her of a sad tale of a lady who became completely addicted and he blamed himself. He lived in dread of hearing she had taken an overdose, though it would have taken three teaspoons to kill her so high was her regular dose – *only two for the likes of you and me,* he had said. As a result of his warnings, she had taken it only a couple of times when her back was bad, a single cautious drop after which she monitored her reactions. It made her feel utterly disconnected from the world, uncaring almost – but the back pain just as bad. She wondered why on earth she had not tipped it down the sink and how long it had lain here forgotten. Doctor Cohen's tricks had returned.

Leaving Dora, who wasn't Dora anymore, to lie in state with a bedside lamp for company, she took the envelopes and the little bottle of laudanum downstairs. She switched off the hall light, picked up Oliver's novel. She passed through the scullery, leaving the laudanum on the draining board, and went into the shop. After collecting her fountain pen, some writing paper and two envelopes from her drawer, she switched off the light and closed the door from the shop to the scullery. She didn't want to attract any attention; she didn't want to be disturbed in any way.

What might William have said to his mother when he got home? Perhaps Mrs Hodge would come bustling down here, partly to feed her own fascination with the fallen and the needy – partly to bristle at the injustice just done to her son. Which Mrs Hodge would arrive? The kind or the cruel? Then there was the matter of Terry's car and the eggs. She imagined he would not be back from his estate agent's office until later. Was Muriel cowering inside? Or perhaps she was out in a rare moment of independence, returning home soon to cook Terry's supper. Beatrix knew she didn't have long till there would be the inevitable knock on the door. She didn't want that – no, she didn't want that.

The scullery was warm, perhaps overly warm. She opened the door to the stove and poked the remaining ashes and coals, which were dampening down after consuming the books. She added her old will to the pyre. Gone in an instant. Settling herself at the table she worked slowly, applying the neatest handwriting she could manage. The kind she used for school.

The Post Office and Sweet Shop
Church Road
Walham Green
Buckinghamshire

To whom it may concern:

Being of sound mind and body this is the last will and testament of Beatrix Alexandra Veal, born in Durham, January 15th, 1887.

I enclose the last will and testament and death certificate for Dora Elizabeth Ham, born in Paris 9th December, 1877. On her death according to her wishes I inherited all her worldly possessions.

I leave all my worldly possessions, bar those that will be claimed by the Westminster and County Bank to honour my debts, to my dear friend Oliver Cope of The Flat, Hodges Butchers, 27 Walkers Lane, Walham Green, Buckinghamshire. He may sell them, dispose of them, or keep them as he sees fit.

Miss Ham left no precise instructions on her funeral, or burial in her will. Should funds be available, as she died of natural causes, I wish her to be afforded a simple ceremony in Walham Church. Following her service, I wish for us both to be cremated. Our ashes are to be combined and scattered without fuss in Carlyle Square in Chelsea, London.

Yours faithfully,
Miss Beatrix Veal
Thursday 18th October 1951

She put her will – she dearly hoped it would be enough to be regarded as a will – and Dora's will with the death certificate into an envelope, sealed it and marked it:

To Whom It May Concern.

She took the second piece of paper.

Thursday 18ᵗʰ October 1951

My Dear Oliver,

I am sorry. You have probably torn up my letter by now – only to have found another.

You will see from my will that I have left you everything. Though I fear that won't be much after the bank has picked their way through the remains. There may be some fuss about criminal damage to Terry Longhurst's car. I do hope not.

I didn't mention Alice in my will. Her telephone number is: DUR 9058. Please ask her not to be hurt by my silence. It seemed way too complicated and frankly parsimonious to hand out valueless trinkets like sweeties. If she would truly like something, then let her choose. I know you will be gracious in this. Perhaps she might like to have my watch? Though I should say that the pearls that I am wearing are Dora's. I suppose they should go to her niece Celeste. A peace offering? Though maybe she wouldn't want them under the circumstances of how they were found. The jet earrings perhaps? They are on the dressing table.

As you know from our conversation this afternoon, I am an atheist, whereas Dora hedged her bets as a life-long agnostic. Dora was only interested in planning her wake – she didn't care about her mortal remains. Having rejected

179

the formality of the church, her relationship was directly with God, if he existed at all. Despite her views the vicar was fond of her. I do hope he will do her the honour of a service at the church (she would appreciate the insurance policy of that) and not feel obliged to make a silly fuss about the illegal manner of my passing and separate our ceremony at the crematorium. It was one of the things that concerned Dora, unlike yours truly. There is talk of reforming the law (if not the view of the church) on suicide. I suppose I must face up to the criminality of my actions in my death. Hopefully the vicar can be persuaded to say a few words through gritted teeth and send us both on our way. Please don't worry and only do what you can and what can be afforded.

We would like our ashes to be mingled and scattered in the place I mentioned today – Carlyle Square – you know it well. There is a bench beside a chestnut tree which would be perfect – but anywhere is fine. I remember we had terrible trouble helping Vera scatter Mary's ashes in Hyde Park – who would have thought anyone might bother with a byelaw – but they did. If it must be done at dead of night for reasons of secrecy that would be very fitting – wouldn't it?

I mentioned the hens and taking them to Greengage's on our walk today. Of course, it would be better they live out their natural days with someone, if they would have them. Apologies, I should have sorted this somehow myself but didn't have the heart.

I will stop organising things now. Nothing more tiresome than a controlling voice from the grave. You will manage it all perfectly.

Once again, I am sorry. I hope, once the initial fury at my rejection of life has worn off, you will understand. The one thing I regret is that I will not find out how my name's sake fares in your books, though I must admit to being mildly put

out that you turned me into a man! Perhaps you could invent
a small, buxom, intelligent, female detective companion for
him to make life more fun. You might not want to use Dora's
surname? Though we always enjoyed introducing ourselves
and watching for the reaction, people might think it cliché.

I don't fear death; nor do I fear the threat of a miserable
afterlife. After all, 'the other place', as Hamlet would have it,
is brightened by the arrival of Persephone each winter. We all
feel immortal till we die.

I am at peace, and I am ready.
Beatrix

She folded the letter into the envelope, wrote Oliver's name
on the front and sealed it with a lick. She left the two envelopes and Oliver's book on the table, one, two, three. She
went to the basement door under the stairs and switched
on the light. The lingering smell of dry-rot from the tiny
cellar below was a constant companion to the steps that led
downwards. She took down the tea-caddy from the spidery
shelf and prized off the lid.

There were a few coins remaining from the last rebate
from the meter man, who unlocked the metal box and
counted the money on the scullery table. After tallying the
value of coins with the quantity of gas used, he would have
Beatrix receive a reasonable return of her own money. Dora
would never meet him – such was her resentment of the
civility required. Beatrix was always civil, though never
grateful. Why should she thank anyone for returning to her
that which was robbed from her in the first place? What a
job. She decided on the fattest: a shilling. She slid the coin
into the slot and turned the large key until she heard the
clunk of the coin into the tin below. It was a careful judgement – she did not want to blow the place to smithereens

and take some unsuspecting passer-by with her. On a whim she took the last remaining coins into the shop, crunched her way across the shattered sweets and broken glass and punched the whole lot into the Barnardo's boy charity box.

Returning to the scullery, she put a small pan of milk onto the stove to heat and turned over the other remaining teacup and saucer on the wooden drainer. She wondered if it were one that Dora had last used. She unlocked the back door and collected a bucket from the wash-house. Returning she took eight sugar cubes from the bowl on the table and crushed them with the back of a spoon from the drawer. The milk now warmed, she added the crushed sugar into the pan, stirring right to the bottom, until every grain was melted. She tasted it, it seemed sweet enough, so she poured it into the teacup.

She picked up the laudanum bottle, shook the contents vigorously and tried to unscrew the cap. It was sealed with age but released its grip after a couple of tries. She squeezed the dropper to make sure all the liquid dripped to the bottom of the bottle. She removed the dropper, took a teaspoon from the draining board, and carefully poured the contents into the spoon, holding it over the teacup in case any drops spilled. She had filled the teaspoon to the brim twice before the bottle gave up; she let the contents slide into the milk. She stirred and stirred and stirred. She was tempted to take just the tiniest of sips to see if it were drinkable, but she feared it might impede her remaining tasks.

The telephone rang. She let it ring. Twenty-three ... twenty-four ... it stopped.

She picked up the pail and drew water from the sink until it was full to the brim. She lifted the hot plate off the stove with the metal tool for the purpose and poured the bucketful into the hot coals below. She repeated this several times, ignoring the fury of the sizzling and popping from deep inside the stove. Steaming water, coal dust and ash began to seep out of the door, then trickle, cooler and faster, as she continued to douse the fire. She stepped back, watching the mess creep over the scullery floor. After the third bucket the stove silenced.

She checked herself and left the back door unlocked – why make things harder than they should be for Oliver? She pulled two bath towels down from the airer that hung above the stove, and ran them under the sink, twisting them into a tight sausage to wring out the surplus water. She picked up the teacup and saucer of poison and the damp towels and left the scullery, flicking out the light and closing the door behind her.

The telephone rang. Twelve ... thirteen ... perhaps it was Underhill's. What to do? She didn't want them arriving, disturbing her. She wanted peace, not this endless ringing. She will put them off till tomorrow – when they will have more than they realised to do. The phone trilled on. She picked up the receiver. Surprisingly she heard pips run on and then silence.

"Hello?" she asked the silent line.

"Beatrix? It's me."

The last person on earth she wanted to speak to now.

"Oliver ... hello. I can't talk now ... I'm so tired. I need to sleep. We'll speak in the morning."

"No. No. I have to speak to you now. Right now, Beatrix. Are you OK?"

"Like I said I am very tired, and I need to get on with things."

"Beatrix listen to me. I have a plan ... you have to forgive me I am a bit squiffy because I've been in the pub for a bit now, but I am deadly, deadly serious about this. I want to put a proposition to you. I haven't thought it through, but whilst I've been here it occurs to me that perhaps you come with me. Perhaps we find a way for us to live in Canterbury together? Something like that might work. I don't really want to live on a farm on my own . . . not my style at all . . . It a great deal closer to London than Durham. Sorry, this is coming out in a bit of muddle."

Beatrix sat down on the chair, switched on the table lamp and rested the teacup and saucer of poison on the table. "Oliver you must stop this now," she said, with all the force she could muster. "This is not a sensible conversation, you're drunk."

"Oh, hang sensible. Sorry, but you should seriously think about what I am saying. You have nowhere to go but a place where you will be utterly miserable."

Beatrix heard herself talking in a perfectly normal manner. "Besides, what would your friends think? Imagine the gossip . . . the scandal," she said, raising her voice in mock horror.

"In all honesty, my cousins won't give a damn. I know them and trust me, they won't. They just want the place sorted so they can retire. Think about it. I will learn, eventually, how to take on the orchard and the small farm business. You can run the cottage and kitchen garden – I mean for goodness' sake there are staff there that can help you when it gets tricky. You can build it back to what it was – even bring the hens! I'll return in the morning first thing. Find out how you are. We can talk some more, put flesh on the bones. I just wanted to tell you tonight, so you had a bit of time to think about it."

"A *mariage blanc*? Is that what you are suggesting? Cover for you and a home for me?"

"Well, I wouldn't go that far! But OK then – companionship of a different kind, I agree."

She laughed. "And you in turn, as I slide into my oldest age, would become the care giver, the garden tenderer, the hen keeper, the egg hunter, the companion that turns one day . . . as I was becoming with Dora . . . that turns into the imprisoned."

"Oh Beatrix, for once let something happen that you just do for the hell of it, for your own sake."

If you only knew, she thought, looking at the rapidly cooling drink by her side. A skin had formed on the surface.

"I am sorry. I don't mean to dismiss your charming, elegant solution lightly. I think the words 'for my sake' would come, in time, to haunt me. I know only too well what it is like to tie your younger self to an increasingly dependent, older other – and you and I were never lovers – love's compensation for the hardest of times. Your writing should be your only dependant now. You don't need me holding you back from a new life and I have no desire to end my days playing the gooseberry . . ." She ran out of words and let the silence hang. It went on so long she almost thought they had been cut off.

"I mean for the fun of it," Oliver finally said, breaking the silence. "I know this is the very last day that you want to hear this, but there is a future. A future for you, if you want to grab it. And besides, you've run out of road."

She felt as exhausted as she had at the kitchen table this morning when Dora said she was changing the plan. Or did she? Then it was hopelessness that exhausted her, now it was fear of her own fallibility, and the unknown. Would it be fun? Could she cope? At the moment of being offered companionship she had never felt so alone.

"That's what I kept saying to Dora. We had . . . now I

185

have . . . run out of road." she said, as tears dripped onto her skirt for the second time today.

"Look, I'm running out of change . . . though I don't want to. Damn it, here come the pips. Listen . . ." he said, pushing more money into the slot as the pips went again, ". . .I am getting an advance on the next two books. The money is coming and soon. Let's tell Miss Moyle to buzz right off tomorrow morning about the damn key, call the bank to stop the bailiffs and think this through properly. I mean it Beatrix, though I am drunk, I would not be suggesting this if I didn't truly mean it. For my own sake as much as yours."

"But it's crazy . . . have you any idea how old I am?"

"There are two types of people in this world Beatrix – the ones who grab at opportunity and the ones who let it pass by. I never had you down as the latter."

"What will we live on?"

"My royalties, your pension and in time the income from the farm and market garden. Canterbury is quite a place you know – they even have a repertory theatre!"

"How far is Canterbury by train from London?" She laughed, and despite everything, it warmed her.

"Now that's more like it," he said. The pips began again. "Beatrix, I've run out of coins. I have to go. I will come first thing. Don't let me down now . . . I need you to help me make this work. You said it yourself. There's always time for one more turn on the roundabout."

She sat in the hall in the pool of light from the little lamp. Could she see her and Oliver in her mind's eye living in a cottage and him helping her with the kitchen garden when her back was too creaky to do it? She would love to nurture another garden. In Oliver there was the potential of a companion who would drop everything for a Shakespeare at the Old Vic, or a lecture on the Greek Gods at the British Museum. They could catch a train up to town – no bombs to fear. She could come to his book launches and watch as he signed the freshly pressed copies of his latest bloody murder stories, adored by a host of little old ladies standing in line, each clutching a hard back copy. Perhaps one would come up to her and ask:

Have you read much of Primus's work? I absolutely adore him.

Yes, in fact we know each other very well. I am his muse. The character of detective Bertie Veal is in fact based on me – and his side-kick Dorinda Ham on my dear friend and companion, now sadly departed.

Well, I am blowed, I had no idea . . . I say, I don't suppose you would also sign my book, would you?

But of course dear . . . and your name..?

When she reached the landing, she switched off the overhead light that had guided her way. She went into the bedroom. The air was still. The room now had a very different aspect to the scullery, but it was a welcome space none the less. She had goosebumps on her arms from the cold. The hair on the back of her head felt tight. She took Dora's cardigan off and hung it over her jacket on the back of the chair. She slipped out of her skirt and blouse, glanced in the mirror and smiled. She took the pins out of her hair and let the plait fall free. One last night. With luck no one would come to the door, and if they did, she would ignore them. After sitting in the hall for a very long time she had poured the laudanum down the kitchen sink and taken the phone off the hook; the shop bell was busted. Peace was all she needed. Tomorrow the new day would come and bring with it whatever it brought.

She sat on the bed and set the alarm clock for six am as always. She took the eiderdown from the chair and lay flat on her back between it and the white top sheet. She tipped her head, resting it on Dora's shoulder. She felt her stomach begin to relax, her feet to warm a little. She breathed deeply, trying to steady her breath. She turned onto her left side in a foetal position, cupped her chin in her left hand, placed her right hand onto Dora's, and closed her eyes – waiting for sleep to come and numb everything out to black. It couldn't take long; her brain ached with anticipation, keen to switch itself off.

"I am coming Dora, but not yet, so forgive me," she said, though she knew Dora could not care one way or the other. She wondered if Dora had felt loved in her last moments; she hoped so.

The bedside clock ticked – what was the time? How long had she been lying there? She imagined what it would have been like to be here having carried out her plan. Perhaps the laudanum would have been too old to work after all? Perhaps the dose not enough? She imagined the gas seeping towards her across the floor, wondered if the fumes would have knocked her out before the pain of the poison took hold – or perhaps it would be better the other way round? Would she have felt her stomach burning? What would breathing in the gas be like if she had still been sentient? Think of something . . . think anything, anything but this, thought Beatrix. Breathe. Breathe.

Girls, are you ready for the fray? Let's go!

Her father is there, standing tall, casting a shadow over the towel. Alice is up with one bound – and taking his hand they run together, ahead of her, down to the sea. She is on her feet and following – minus the rubber ring that Alice inherited – on her long and lanky, pipe-cleaner legs; 'long' she understands – but what did 'lanky' mean? The cold water hits her reluctant limbs and shortens her stride, if it could be shortened any further, such is her lack of desire to be in the ice-cold sea. Her costume clings to her knees; she is feeling the drag of it in the waves that pull and push her about. Alice and her father are jumping the waves ahead. Ah, the joy of it for them, the torture for her. She draws level and lowers her body into the foam. Her jaw is clenching. Breathe, breathe, through the cold, but her held-in stomach squashes her lungs, making that harder and harder. She can feel her skin tingle, her arms are heavy in the water, the force of it making them hard to move. Soon the terror of the swim will be over – think of the warmth of the towel, the creamy chocolate square, the wrist watch to come ...

"Come my duck – come Beatrix, now it's your turn, do your level best." Her father's voice is calm and reassuring.

She can see Alice safely in the shallows. She can feel the warmth of his body in the water next to hers. She can lean on him, and he will be there. In her stomach it feels warm but she is shivering with the cold. Strong arms are around her – all his wiry attention is hers.

"Hold my hands and let your legs float up. That's it, you are a cork bobbing on the ocean. If you believe it, you will float. See. See how your legs come up to the surface if you just believe that they will. Relax. We all float if we have faith ... Relax, just relax, and believe and you will float. That's it, that's it, open your eyes."

She opens her eyes a tiny slit. The world has turned blue; the sea stretches out in all directions, blue sea meeting blue sky; her body is never still for a minute, she is wriggling rather than swimming, but he doesn't seem to mind. The bright reds, greens and yellows of other swimmers' bathing caps float on her horizon. She lets go of his hands and tries to kick her heavy legs.

"In through the nose and out through the mouth." She does as he says, and it eases her panic. "One, two, three . . ." he is calling the numbers of breaststrokes; she swims as if her life depended on it. "Seven, eight, nine . . . twenty Beatrix, only twenty and you've proved you can swim . . . twelve, thirteen, fourteen . . . eyes open, mouth closed – you silly – I love you so much you stubborn, stubborn child," and he shouts to a beat like a sergeant major, "eyes open, mouth closed." She can feel her legs want to drop beneath the surface, her head want to come up . . . "in through the nose, and out through the mouth, eyes open, mouth closed . . . seventeen, eighteen, nineteen . . . keep breathing . . . keep swimming . . . twenty . . . you did it! You did it!"

She closes her eyes tight. Her freed arms begin to flail. Her breathing is fast, the panic setting in, the water is too thin to hold her, way too thin, she is falling, dropping, her legs leave off any attempt to find the surface and try to find the sand below. Her mouth is wide open as the rising sea over-takes her, she is gulping for air, choking, the water rushes in over her head. She can hear his voice more distant now . . . "eyes open . . . mouth closed," but she can't do that, she can't do that . . . that never would work now, as she breathes in the ocean, the brine filling her lungs. Her heart is pumping fast, she can feel it pulsing in her chest, the whooshing noise from the sea is in her ears.

Her lungs are full. So full in fact that it dawns on her now that breathing is no longer a problem. Far better to just relax and let herself go. As she calms, she begins to enjoy the sensation. No more fear, nothing to worry about. Down, down, down through the thin water she drops, feet first. She spins slowly round, looking at the passing underwater world of endless refracted light. Jet streams of bubbles pass her by on their way to the surface – released from somewhere below. There is all the air that is needed in this place. Just in that moment in a way that is as surprising as it is expected, her mother joins her, dropping downwards alongside. She mirrors the slow free-fall spin, wrapping her arms around Beatrix, holding her, not asking her to breathe because she is breathing. Breathing in water feels so much easier than on land, calming; this is a peaceful place. Her mother's arms hug her close. The two of them revolve in a slow dance, their heads touching, their arms supporting each other. She is safe. She knows she did her level best to be everything to everyone, she is released from any sense of burden. She lifts her knees up to her tummy, she is warm, she is cradled, and nothing, nothing, nothing else matters ... but this.

Historical Note

As Dora and Beatrix knew, the women's suffrage movement had its factions. Millicent Fawcett's National Union of Women's Suffrage Societies formed in 1897 (suffragists). Christabel and Emmeline Pankhurst's Women's Social and Political Union formed in 1903 (suffragettes). A key difference between them was the suffragist rejection of violence or illegal tactics.

Beatrix's non-establishment work contract was a mechanism for protecting jobs for returning soldiers. Villiage sub-post offices formed a significant part of the war effort – letters to and from the front line being a vital boost to morale. Temporary (non-establishment) roles offered no employment protection or pension when the push for modernisation and restructure of the postal service happened at the end of the Second World War.

Dora's left-handed change was common action for a child at the turn of the century; being left-handed was considered a sign of disadvantage. As a result, children were denied the use of their dominant hand, causing what must have been endless frustration.

The Gateways Club, 239 Kings Road, opened in 1931 and closed its green door in 1985. Much loved by the LGBTQ+ community it became women only in 1967, and was enjoyed as a haven by the lesbian community – particularly after their eviction from the Bag O'Nails pub close by. Run from 1943 by the triangle of Ted Ware, his wife Gina and manager Smithy, it was determinedly non-political – but drinking, smoking, dancing, dressing up and flirting were actively encouraged.

I apologise that Mr Wilkins causes offence by his out-dated racial description when describing the heroism of the 6888th Central Postal Directory Battalion, also known as the Six Triple Eight, whose current website describes them as "multi-ethnic, predominantly Black with one Mexican and one Puerto Rican woman". In 1945 these 855 heroines rescued 17 million letters and parcels stranded in Birmingham UK and delivered them to US troops and families. They were awarded the Congressional Gold Medal in 2021.

Acknowledgements

I would like to thank the following:

For help and inspiration: Duncan Campbell-Smith for his book *Masters of the Post* and Jill Gardiner for *From the Closet to the Screen: Women at the Gateways Club 1945-1985*.

For brilliant instruction: Francis Spufford, Maura Dooley and James Scudamore.

For robust feedback and care: The Angels writers' group, my editor Dawn Howarth, Susie Sainsbury, Greg Mosse, Jo Melling, Leah Schmidt, Neil Barlett, Lucy Ellis, Pip Broughton, Carol Clark and my other early readers.

For their unstinting belief: my husband Clive; children Thomas, Paul, Sam, Annie, Jack, Harry and Grace; my sister Pam; Liubov Sliusareva, Lavinia Thomas, Nicky Jones and my publishers Sarah and Kate Beal of Muswell Press.

Finally, in thanks to my Mum, Jill Taylor, who never knew how far this got, but encouraged me to write, told me of the existence of the shopkeepers Miss Veal and Miss Ham and germinated an idea in the corner of my mind, from which this whole fantastical story grew.

A Note on the Author

Vikki Heywood was Executive Director of the Royal Shakespeare Company from 2003 until 2012 and before that Joint Chief Executive of the Royal Court Theatre. She has been an executive producer of many West End and Broadway productions, including Matilda the Musical. She was Chairman of the RSA 2012-2018, and in 2020 was awarded a Damehood for services to the Arts. This is her first novel.

www.vikkiheywood.com
@damevikkiheywood